THAT NIGHT & OTHER STORIES

That Night & Other Stories
By Peter F. Crowley
Published by CAAB Publishing Ltd
(Reg no 12484492)

C . A . A . B
PUBLISHING

5 Brayford Sq, London, UK
www.caabpublishing.co.uk

First Published 2023
1 3 5 7 9 10 8 6 4 2

Printed in the UK
British Library Cataloguing in Publication data available

i

Table of Contents

Introduction

Unlike many writers, who may craft their stories or novel over a sudden "burst of energy" while a writer-in-residence at an esteemed university, or who have been bankrolled by their parents or an inheritance, or a lucrative publication contract, this work was crafted by the slow, laborious animal of time. The stories were concocted while working a full-time job in the information science industry and, for the past few years, fathering a young child. The flash fiction pieces and short stories that appear here were written when hours could be pulled away from constant busyness. I would steal away quietly to the basement, sit at my typewriter, with coffee or tea, and let "the flow" do the rest. Thus, this collection of stories may feel a bit disparate, consisting of various styles and themes that I've been toying with over the years. They have been inspired by different elements of life that affected me at the time when I sat down at the typewriter, ranging from sociopolitical dystopia and satire ("That Night," "The Real United States" and others), interpersonal conflicts ("Tumbleweed," "Dump" and more) to more whimsical pieces like "The Romantic" and "All the Time in the World."

I welcome you to read these one at a time, by randomly opening the book and selecting the story that you land on, or to go with a more traditional cover-to-cover reading. The styles that you will find here, of course, have this author's hallmark and technique of writing, but do vary quite a bit, from more straightforward realism, to surrealism, symbolism and magic realism.

This book is dedicated to my two-year-old son, Wally. May you go forth with openness, intelligence and creativity into the increasingly myopic world. In addition to heightened xenophobia, the world that you are slowly getting to know is beset by the risks of climate change, nuclear war, increasingly powerful AI and reduced biodiversity. Continue on in the state of perpetual *becoming*, with clarity of vision and fortitude.

I'd like to offer a deep thank you to all my friends and family who have helped along the way. My wife Priyanka Kabir, PhD, democracy scholar and research analyst, has tirelessly provided feedback on many of these stories. A pandemic writer's group, consisting of author and PhD candidate Stephen Waldron, poet Linda Werbner and musician/lyricist Dan Morse, have all offered insightful feedback to many of these stories.

x

Initials

In my parent's cellar, on the black water pipes running parallel to the ceiling, the previous owner's son hung themselves. His parents had gone away and come home to find him. He was in his early 20s. My father told me that when they first were shown the house, the son's friends were shooting up heroin in the finished basement area.

We moved in a month later, just before I turned three.

In my senior year of high school, I smoked pot heavily, usually by myself. Whenever high alone, I avoided going into the cellar, particularly to the unfinished part where the suicide occurred. A few times, I faced my unconscious fear and sat down underneath the pipes to debunk my belief in ghosts as an aspiring existential rationalist. I wouldn't admit it to myself then, but there was a kind of darkness to the unfinished basement.

Not so long ago, I received a call from an unknown number. As usual, I rejected it, sending it to voicemail. The same number called again a few minutes later. Again, I ignored it. Shortly later my phone vibrated, indicating a voicemail had been left. I listened, expecting to hear an automated fraud message. Instead, it was a woman's voice that sounded vaguely familiar.

"Sorry to bother you, Mr. Flaherty, but this is the current resident of 15 Powhatan Road in Blackstone. My husband and I ate to disturb you, but we have a few questions about the house. Could you please return our call at 781-254-2333? Thanks so much! Jill."

Strange, I thought. My parents had moved out a few years ago to live in a smaller place that required less upkeep. I had never met the new buyers or heard anything about them.

I waited a few hours and returned their call.

A man with a deep, serious voice answered.

"Hello. Could I please speak to Jill?"

"Who is this?"

"This is someone who used to live at 15 Powhatan. And I believe Jill contacted me regarding that."

His voice suddenly warmed.

"Oh, yeah, of course. Jill's my wife. We live where you used to live and wanted to talk to you about the house. It's…" His voice trailed off.

"Hello? Can you still hear me? I'm not sure if the line was cut. Hello?"

After a few moments, a woman's voice came on.

"Hi Mr. Flaherty, this is Jill. Is it possible that we meet in person? It's just that the line seems to be breaking and there's a lot to cover."

"Is this about property damage? Or maybe a purchasing agreement? If so, I think either my parents or your realtor would be best to contact."

"No," Jill responded, pausing, "we already contacted your parents, but they thought you'd be the best person to talk to."

Reluctantly, I agreed to meet them for coffee at a Starbucks near my old house. It was a very busy month for me, as a marketing director of Solvent, an AI firm that develops deep learning algorithms to detect Alzheimer's years before traditional diagnosis.

Immediately upon walking into Starbucks, a couple waved to me from the corner. As they stood to shake my hand, they each looked to be around 5 feet tall, with Jill slightly taller than her husband. They were probably in their mid-40s. He was muscular with a goatee, and she was an attractive blonde with year-round tan skin. I mention this because it was February in New England when I met them.

As we talked, it soon became apparent that they had also heard the story of the young man committing suicide in their basement nearly 35 years ago and were trying to get answers anywhere they could. They also added, as a side note, that they were fans of the "Ghost Hunters" tv show and seemed to suggest that their basement may be haunted. But had they sought an appointment with my siblings or parents? Why were they so interested in having an in-depth meeting with me?

After describing noises that they heard emanating from the basement in the middle of the night, they asked me about my past. They seemed to want a full bio – how long did I live in that house? Did I hang out in the basement often? Did I ever hear strange noises from there? When did I move in and when did I leave? And so on. I tried to answer them briefly with as little information as possible, as it slowly began to feel a bit like an interrogation.

The conversation seemed to be dwindling, as I was unwilling to offer much detailed personal information to complete strangers.

For a few minutes, they changed the subject to the weather, Red Sox spring training and the team's prospects for the coming season. It felt like they were trying to find ways to buy time.

Jill placed her hand on my wrist, as if doing so would extract further information.

"Did you ever write your initials anywhere in the basement?"

I thought back for a second.

"No, never."

The man squinted and gave me a hard look.

"Mr. Flaherty, are you being honest with us?"

"Yeah, of course."

They remained dubious, so I continued, "I mean, I spray-painted a couple of band names on the front walkway, like Rancid. But I don't think I've ever written my initials anywhere besides when signing forms."

"You're lying!" the man blurted out.

"Honey, relax," Jill said, placing both hands gently on his shoulder.

"Your initials are CFF, right?" she inquired.

I nodded.

"Those initials are deeply scrawled into the basement cement."

My jaw hung open. I thought for a second. "It could always be that someone with the same initials lived there before me. Or maybe CFF stands for something else – like a group or organization?"

Jill took out her iPhone and showed me the picture of the unfinished basement and zoomed in on the initials. It *was* CFF.

"OK, well, you've convinced me. They're there. But I never saw them the whole time I lived there. And I definitely did not write them."

As we parted, they seemed to believe me and said they would continue further research on municipal records to see who lived there previously.

While intrigued, I wondered aloud why it was such a big deal that they uncover who wrote it.

"You don't seem to understand," the man began, "every night we hear noises from the basement. When we go down there and shine a flashlight on those initials, it stops."

I grinned, shaking my head.

"Have you replaced the old furnace yet? I remember that would always make a hell of a lot of noise."

In a solemn, measured tone, the husband retorted, "This is not a joke, Mr. Flaherty, this is our lives. This is where we live! We can't sleep. We need to get some peace!"

"OK, well, why don't you guys go ahead and do some research and let me know what you find."

It was a while until I heard from them again. The weather was warm, air conditioners were humming. It was early July.

They asked to meet again at the Starbucks near their house.

When I met them, they seemed visibly distraught. The woman's once-tanned skin was pallor and the man seemed to have lost a substantial amount of weight. The whites of his serious eyes shone out in panic from his gaunt face.

They cut right to the chase.

After getting coffees, Jill alleged, "Mr. Flaherty, there's something you're not telling us."

"What do you mean? I was kind enough to divulge much of my past to each of you, perfect strangers, back in February. Honestly, I don't know what you two are after!"

They exchanged glances. Jill began to speak, but her husband put his hand up.

In a slow, deliberate tone, as if premeditated, he said, "Mr. Flaherty, we have been completely forthcoming with you, about our home, our problems with the basement and the mysterious initials. We looked up the municipal records online, then went to City Hall to confirm. And then even reached out to the remaining relatives of…"

"Don't act like you don't know!" Jill interrupted in a shrill voice. "You're the bastard who's keeping us awake!"

Anger seethed in her eyes and her husband tried to calm her.

"Basically, the gig is up," the man said, "CFF is Christopher Francis Flaherty. The name of the young man who killed himself in 1982. That is you!"

Abruptly, the woman took out a spray can, which had GHOST FIGHTER written in large red letters on its side and shot a biting mist into my eyes. For ten minutes or so, I couldn't see anything and felt a throbbing chili pepper-type of sting. A Starbucks barista dabbed a cold wet cloth on my eyes. By the time I could see again, the police had arrived, and the couple were gone.

The police implored me to provide them with comprehensive information about the couple. I told the cops that they were mentally disturbed, and that I'd rather refrain from giving any personal information about them. This drew suspicion. They cajoled me for more information so they could talk to the couple and have a record of the incident, even if I didn't want to press charges.

I explained that I just wanted to put the incident behind me and go home to recover.

They let me go, saying that they would contact me in a few days.

After a long nap and shower, I sat down to watch the Red Sox.

Grabbing my laptop, I typed in "Blackstone municipal records."

It cost $40 to gain access. I immediately accepted.

And then I saw it.

15 Powhatan Road, born 1961, died 1982.
Christopher Francis Flaherty.

Alissa

Alissa is late to spend the day at her sister Margaret's nonprofit.

Her light brown hair is tucked behind her ears. She wears a black business suit with red slacks and a silver, semi-reflective, heart-shaped locket that Margaret gave her as a birthday gift when she turned fifteen.

"Maybe a bit overdressed," Alissa thinks as she looks into the closet door mirror, "but that's all I got."

It was either that or an old sweater and jeans, the kind that she wears to her own office, Orcos, where she designs AI software.

Walking inside Wellington Station, a whitish-chalky dust hovers in the air and causes Alissa to cough. As she takes the escalator to the lower level, she finds no one waiting for the T. Something clicks: services have been reduced. She waits for over twenty minutes, checking her phone watch repeatedly. It's already 10:40 am – how did it get so late?

Taking a deep breath, she goes back outside and looks for a taxi. They are lined up waiting for passengers but there are no drivers inside. Towards the end of the taxi queue, two older black men chat with each other. She waves to them, giving a distinct nod; they wave back and continue chatting.

In the parking lot, a car is idling. An older gray-haired woman sits in the driver's seat.

"Must be an Uber," Alissa thinks as she walks up to the car.

"Can I get a ride to Boston – 25 Alder Street?"

The woman gestures for her to get in.

A tall, older man, with a bald crown and gray hair around the sides, sits in the front passenger seat.

The older couple greets her in an Eastern European accent. Alissa knows that there is something that she should be remembering but can't quite recall what it is.

As they drive, she gazes out the window. Route 99 towards Boston is ghostly, store fronts are either dark or shuttered, few cars pass, and she sees only one pedestrian walking and peering anxiously from side to side. At a red light, she looks at a newly renovated McDonalds. Inside the lights are on, but it is empty. When the light turns green, she sees a long line of cars trailing around the drive-thru window.

"Where is everyone?" Alissa asks the couple.

"It is almost 11 in the morning, things are quiet around this time," the man says, looking back to Alissa.

A second later he looks back at her with squinted eyes, as if discovering something new and revealing about her.

Nearing Charlestown, the right turn onto the interstate is backed up. All along the highway entrance and on 93 South, cars are stuck in gridlock traffic. Straight ahead, in the direction of the North End, the road is completely vacant.

The driver makes an abrupt swerve and pulls into the traffic going onto 93 South.

"I almost missed the turn!" the woman says, glancing back to Alissa through the rear-view mirror.

"I'll never get there in time now. Why didn't you just go straight?"

"I couldn't! But no problem, we'll get you there soon."

The driver turns off the car ignition in the middle of traffic.

The couple gets out and the man opens the door for Alissa.

"Yes, leave it to us," he says.

Alissa follows them across the street and under the interstate overpass, where, amidst overgrown grass, empty liquor bottles and cigarette butts, is an opening leading underground.

As they descend a few hundred feet, the man says, "This tunnel was built in the early 20th century. They had thought this would be a subway line, but it never happened."

A familiar whitish chalky dust pervades the air. They cough a bit and Alissa's throat becomes parched.

After walking for a while, the older man turns to Alissa and extends his hand.

"How rude of me. I'm Ivan."

"Alissa. Nice to meet you."

With a wide smile, the woman turns to her and says, "I am Gretchen."

"Nice meeting you."

Gretchen, shorter and stouter than Alissa, embraces her and says in her ear, "Nice to meet you, too. We'll get through this."

While this all feels perfectly natural to Alissa, she has the feeling that this kind of behavior shouldn't be done for some reason. But, why, she couldn't remember. Also, what was there to get through?

As they continue walking along in the dimly lit tunnel, they come upon an intersection.

Gretchen's and Ivan's faces look confused as they speak to each other in Croatian.

"You will stay here," Gretchen says to Alissa.

In response to Alissa's confusion, Ivan says, "As you see, there are several tunnels and none of them are labeled. Some lead up to the city and others just continue on like this, forever. We'll go find the one that leads aboveground near Alder Street, as you wish."

They leave Alissa for what seems like an eternity.

Suddenly, Ivan's distant voice says, "You don't have to do this. Don't hurt me! Don't..."

"Shut up!" a gruff male voice says.

Alissa hears something heavy fall to the ground on what seems to be a higher level of the tunnel.

"Where's Gretchen?" Alissa wonders as she starts sprinting through the tunnel's chalky dust.

After what seems like forever and her mouth has become parched by the tunnel's chalky dust, Alissa finds a narrow stairway. Upon reaching the top, she opens a heavy, steel door and emerges onto East India Street near downtown.

"Civilization, at last!" Alissa thinks. "Wait 'til I tell Margaret and the people at the office about this!"

Glancing at her phone, she sees that it's already noon. The streets are empty, void of the usual parade of lunch-goers. Only the dark, sleeping buildings watch over her, curious to see what she will do next.

"Maybe there are people inside looking out too." she thinks. "But if they are, they're hidden by the windows' shadows."

She walks down East India Street, takes a right on Milk Street, and comes to Alder. A sense of accomplishment fills Alissa as she walks slowly towards No. 25.

25 Alder has a large, ornate lobby, where typically a receptionist would be seated for visitors to check-in. But when she looks in, the lights are off, and the receptionist's desk is empty. Alissa bangs on the locked door, but there is no sign of movement inside. Then she goes to the small loading dock at the side of the building, but that door is also locked.

Alissa returns to the front and peers in; her hands cup her eyes to block the light from either side to gain full visibility, but it still looks completely empty. She sits down, looks through her phone and texts her sister.

As she awaits a response, Alissa hears a knock on the glass window behind her. The janitor, a middle-aged, balding white man, begins talking to her, but the thickness of the building's glass prevents his voice from being audible.

From the intensity of his eyes, he seems to be saying something important. He points to the mottled brown office building across the street. Alissa shrugs and walks over to 22 Alder.

Standing at the door of No. 22, she mouths back to the janitor, "This one?"

The janitor nods.

Alissa rings the bell and bangs on the front door. Inside, the reception area is dim and vacant. No one answers.

She takes a deep breath and turns back across the street.

The janitor has disappeared.

Her phone vibrates with a message from Margaret.

It says, "Alissa, I had been expecting you to visit me at the office for a long time now. I invited you last year on this very day. But you've come at the wrong time. A time when the wind has taken humanity and left only dust.

P.S., I now work remotely. We all do. Where have you been all this time?"

That Night

She looked in the mirror and put lipstick on. Her lips curled up in a slight sneer. Her eyes met their own reflection and, following an infinite bounding back and forth of gazing into themselves, her confidence burgeoned defiantly, much like a regrown olive tree near Bethlehem.

"You can do it!" Sarah told herself in a quiet, determined voice.

An hour later, she was near downtown Chicago, stuck in a late rush-hour traffic jam. Her car heater was on full blast, as the night was like many others in that Chicago winter: wind chills that plummeted the temperature far below zero.

Sarah turned on the car radio. NPR's Jane Clayson was asking a guest about Donald Trump's 2018 State of the Union address, particularly about his drug pricing policy and its relationship with his campaign rhetoric. Clayson mentioned that during his campaign, Trump had lambasted the pharmaceutical industry but recently appointed a pharma industry executive as Health and Human Services director.

For a minute or two, Sarah tried hard to listen meticulously, to avert her mind from the traffic, and more importantly, the momentous night ahead. Realizing that she was not actually listening but, instead, daydreaming, she turned off the radio.

It was now 6:20 pm. Her speech was in less than an hour at 7:15, about 3 miles away by the Marquette Building. With traffic, that could take over a half hour.

Her phone rang.

"Hi Sarah, where are you?"

It was Jim, her assistant. He had helped her teach a class on gender during the fall semester and listened patiently as she practiced delivering her speech.

"Damn it, Jim – I'm stuck in traffic! I may not get there until seven!"

"Holy shit!" Jim responded, then paused, his mind whirling as he considered how he could help remedy the situation. For a second, too, he chastised himself for swearing so readily with his superior, with whom he usually held a more formal relationship.

"I could see if the organizer can put you on at a later slot?" he suggested.

Sarah began to feel heavy drops of sweat falling down the sides of her stomach. She turned the heat down and pensively wiped her forehead.

"No, we can't do that – that will foul up the whole night. Just, please, make sure everything's ready to go when I get there."

"Ok…but," Jim began to say before realizing that she had hung up. What he was going to say was that, since Sarah had the computer with the PowerPoint slides, there wasn't much he could do in the interim. However, he could warn the organizer that Sarah was stuck in gridlock traffic and might be a couple of minutes behind schedule.

Sarah turned the radio back on and flipped through stations. AKCT, classical – exactly what she needed right now.

"Is this Beethoven or Bach?" She mused.

Sarah pushed her seat back and slouched down, trying to relax. After a minute or two of Bach, or Beethoven, she turned off the radio, finding little solace in early 19th-century music.

Seconds later she turned the radio back on and flipped to classical rock. Robert Plant was singing, "In the days of my youth, I had learned what it means to be a man…"

"And what pray tell is that? Sex? Drugs? Rock n' roll?" she muttered, then laughed to herself.

Up ahead was McCormick Place, where she was to deliver her speech "Gender in the Internet Era."

As Sarah drew closer, she could see Jim pacing by the front door. When she pulled up, she rolled down the window.

"Here, let me park this for you," he suggested.

She gave him the keys, grabbed her laptop case from the passenger seat and walked briskly through the entrance doors. It was now 6:50.

Sarah found her way to the back of the stage where Gedine, the event organizer, looked relieved to see her.

"I heard about the traffic – I was worried you weren't going to make it!"

"Yeah, sorry about that. I should've known that'd happen and left earlier."

"Well, you're here now," Gedine said reassuringly.

Sarah went to a side room, where she opened her laptop and started running through the slides for her presentation.

"Sarah," Gedine said, her face contorting with concern as she slowly walked towards her. Sarah glanced up, her face mirroring the unease of Gedine's countenance.

"I've noticed that there are some in the crowd who look a bit off – like they don't quite seem like they belong here."

"Corporate types? They probably wanted to find a decent educational or research conference to attend for a tax write off."

"No, *they* aren't who I had in mind," Gedine responded gingerly.

"Then, who?" Sarah grinned, "Did a bunch of homeless people sneak in?"

"No. It seems, well, I don't know, there are a lot of young men whose haircuts may indicate they're white nationalists or from the 'alt-right'."

"White nationalists?" Sarah asked, chuckling nervously. "What would they be doing here? Tonight's topic isn't even on race at all...and it's not about Donald Trump either!"

"That's true. But recently they've been pushing back against gender studies events, especially those held by universities. They say it's all a waste of money and supposedly suffocating the country with political correctness. Also, we've got a few anonymous calls..."

Sarah stared blankly ahead. She had not, in a million years, thought that white nationalists would attend her speech in protest.

"What do you think they'll do? Take notes or try to interrupt?" Sarah inquired cautiously.

"I really don't know...hopefully nothing. And we can always call security if they do."

Jim entered the back room.

"I just parked the car." He pointed to his watch, "It's 7:15 – you're up!"

Sarah took her laptop and entered the stage. At the center, she placed a laptop on a podium, plugged it in and took a few minutes to set up.

Then she glanced to the side. Gedine gave her a thumbs-up to begin.

"Good evening, ladies and gentlemen," she began, noticing that the lights which illuminated her on the stage had also blinded her view of the audience. "...tonight, I will go through my research on gender and Internet culture, including the Internet's creation of new norms, theories of knowing from a gender studies perspective and complicating what gender means in the Internet Age. Then I will attempt to answer what the consequential implications are for the future."

She went to her first slide, which showed a young woman using Facebook.

"Now the Internet has offered an array of social outlets onto which both men and women project their identity, both the one which they project into the 'real world' and a different kind of identity that does not entirely sync with their 'real world'…"

A strident voice suddenly yelled out, interrupting her, "Hey bitch, shave your legs!" The young white man who had intervened was standing up; one could see the shaved sides of his head, with brown gelled hair on top that was combed to the side. He was well-dressed and looked like someone one may see at an Ivy League school.

Sarah paused; consternation evinced her countenance.

Another young man stood up beside him and bellowed out, "If you don't like our country, go back to Russia, you commie!"

Then yet another young man stood out, calling out, "Hippie slut, we don't care about your PC gender research! Go home!"

Additional young white men, with similar dress and haircuts as the first man, stood up, each with their own voluble declamation.

Two unarmed security guards tried to lead the 15 men out, but they were overpowered. After shouting their individual tirades, they started clamoring in unison, "No gender studies from hippie sluts!"

During this time, Sarah's face had flushed red, while remaining on stage, a bit stupefied. She had no idea what to do. She vaguely asked the audience, "Will someone please escort these men out?" But the young men's chants had muffled her plea.

From the side of the stage, Gedine mouthed to Sarah, with phone in hand, "I'm going to call the police."

Sarah nodded eagerly, then shrugged, mouthing back, "What should I do?"

The white nationalists' chants didn't stop until the police arrived twenty minutes later and escorted them out.

By then Sarah's time slot for speaking was over. Though Gedine insisted that Sarah continue with her lecture, Sarah was in no mood to do so.

She ended up sitting through two of her colleagues' lectures. Towards the end of the second lecture, she dejectedly mused, "If only I had gone on later, there would be no problem. I guess that's luck for you!"

When she arrived home, her husband Jared was watching tv.

"How did the night go, honey?"

"Absolutely horrible! I was heckled off the stage!"

"What? You're kidding, right?" he asked, getting up and looking closely at her face, which began to sadden, her eyes welling with tears.

"No, I'm not! Some group of white nationalists or alt-righters showed up and started saying all these demeaning things towards me."

Tears began to roll down her cheeks. Disbelief deluged Jared's face, for a second, he studied Sarah's face to see if she was playing a joke on him.

As he walked closer to her, he could see that her tears were real.

"I can't believe it! Those fucking bastards! I'll find them and give them a piece of my mind!" He exclaimed as he walked towards her and took her in his arms.

After they embraced for a few minutes, Sarah went upstairs to see her three-year-old son Jeremy sleeping.

Jared came in behind her.

"He looks like a sleeping angel," Sarah whispered in his ear.

Jared smiled and nodded quietly.

Sarah went into the bathroom to wash her makeup off before bed. After clearing her face, she looked in the mirror at her eyes, her reflection shooting back and forth an infinite number of times, like a blitzkrieg pinball. Her mouth tightened, and her countenance became stoic.

She stayed like this for a bit, losing track of time.

Then, she looked in her eyes again. A shiver went down her spine as she straightened her posture.

A lazy smile evinced from her countenance.

Sarah thought to herself, "What bad, no, shit-bad, luck. But, if I can stand through that barrage and not run from the stage or crumble before the crowd, I can stand through anything."

When she lay down in bed beside Jared, he asked, "Want me to file a complaint or let the newspaper know the kinds of travesties these racists are pulling?"

Sarah turned towards him, with the side of her head resting on the pillow. He wondered why she now looked so fresh, beautiful and content after such a rough night.

"What I want you to do is...*absolutely* nothing."

"But...why not? They deserve to be punished or publicly rebuked for this stunt."

"Of course, they do," Sarah responded in a calm voice and self-assured smile. "But that's not the point. They want to gain traction through publicity. The more publicity they have, the more they become an accepted staple of everyday life. We want those cowardly creatures to go back into the hole that they crawled out from."

Jared looked upwards through the bedroom's darkness towards the ceiling.

After a minute, he looked back at her, "I get it."

Platypus

One morning there was a platypus walking through our backyard. I awoke my wife and suggested that we take some photographs. She agreed and perched herself by the window, ready to snap pictures on her phone.

"Why don't you go outside?" I suggested. "You'll probably get a better shot out there."

She looked at me, not without a mild dose of trepidation, "But, what if it bites? Are they known to be dangerous to people?"

I smiled, musing aloud, "There's no such thing as a dangerous 'wild animal'. It's people who pose the greatest danger to themselves."

We went to the edge of our back porch to get as close as possible to the platypus that was now scouring the ground for insect larvae. For a short while, it seemed to take little notice of us, except for emitting an initial befuddled grunt as we stepped outside.

But after Sarah whispered to me, "Maybe we could keep it as our pet," the animal looked up at us with consternation – it was now the fearful one – before brusquely turning around and disappearing behind the brush at the edge of our backyard.

"Let's follow it!" Sarah exclaimed, like some sort of expedition leader. I shrugged and went along with her.

After making our way through the dense copse of trees and brush on our backyard's border, we emerged into an empty verdant meadow. The platypus had vanished.

We trudged back to the house in downtrodden mien. Our dreams and fantasies, encapsulated in a matter of minutes, of the possibilities of having a pet platypus had come to naught. The rest of the day seemed laden with vacuity. Our lives had returned to the boredom of everyday reading, work, eating, gardening and drinking alcohol. It seemed that the potential of having a platypus had eclipsed our lives in such a profound way that, unknowingly, we had invested our all into this. Without the platypus, our lives were undiscovered lithic fragments at an archaeological site or bluestones from prehistoric Welsh quarries, forgotten on their journey to the druids' Stonehenge masterpiece. Without the platypus, we would not depict astronomy as had the druids, nor harvest wild wheat on the Hilly Flanks. Instead, the two of us were confined to our house of fixated time.

--

Each day after that, we gazed out our back window, a vast hope welling within us. And, each day there were none, other than sparrows, robins, chipmunks and an occasional muskrat passing by.

We started to give up hope.

One morning I woke up to a shriek.

"A burglar? Had my wife taken a fall?" I wondered, rushing down the stairs.

The house was empty. I opened the front door; there was nothing.

Then, another shriek, followed by, "Come here Joe! I caught him! Help me bring him inside!"

I bolted to the backyard and saw my wife struggling to contain the platypus in a see-through plastic trash bag.

"What the hell are you doing?" I asked, thinking my wife had gone completely mad.

"Get some rope!" she ordered, ignoring my question.

"No, we can't do this! What are we going to do with him?"

"We will keep him! He'll have a nice life with us," she responded, not looking up as she tried to press the platypus's bill into the bag.

"This is ridiculous. Let the animal go!"

The platypus was starting to break through the plastic bag. It succeeded and my wife was struggling to keep it from moving. I don't remember what got into me, but suddenly I sprinted towards the house, went inside to grab something and was back to where Sarah had been struggling with the platypus in less than a minute.

Yet they were both gone. I saw some movement through the copse at the end of the backyard and ran in that direction. In the meadow behind our yard, Sarah was following the platypus, cajoling it, "Come on, my platypus, we won't hurt you..."

The platypus was not moving very quickly but looked pretty angry. Then I jumped on it, contained it and we succeeded in tying it up with rope.

"Let's put it in the basement, for now at least," I suggested as we carried it towards the house.

Eventually, we got a cage for the animal, named him Cam and kept it in our living room. We learned from some online research that platypuses were highly intelligent and could be used by humans for many things like assisting with unspoken interpersonal communication through their reading of visual cues, as de facto insect repellants and, once well-trained, could even perform special deliveries on holidays if the recipient was instructed to give the platypus a good tip with a food that they like, such as shrimp or crayfish. Our platypus learned to do all this but seemed to do much more – what's more, is hard to explain, and I can't put my finger on it. But it has certainly changed our lives forever and I cannot imagine what our lives would be like without him. It would probably be like living in the Dark Ages or something.

To be honest, some days we don't leave the house anymore. It's either a weekend or Sarah and I are both supposed to be working from home and end up sitting on the couch in front of the platypus's cage, staring at the animal. If someone were to glance through our window during these extended time periods, they would likely see a man and wife gaping, almost stupefied with their mouths slightly ajar, at a wild animal in a cage. But certainly, it is more than this. Hours dissipate, melting like Dali's surreal clocks. This animal seems to transform all the extra space in our lives, where once rested doubts, misgivings, anxieties and it disintegrates them. I can't tell you how or why this happens...it just kind of happens!

These days some critics will say that pets can exert substantial and even detrimental control over their owners. Yet I know that's not true and probably only happens in the rarest of cases.

However, on *occasion* this may happen to us. For example, on a Friday night not long ago, Sarah and I were supposed to go out to dinner with another couple whom we've long known. The platypus seemed to watch us get ready with intense curiosity. As we neared the front door to leave, the platypus bleated a call of distress.

"Oh!... Cam is upset that we're going out...Maybe we should just stay here?" Sarah asked, frowning.

"No way," I answered, point-blank. "We have plans - let's keep them."

She nodded and we got into the car. But Sarah looked towards the house. "I can still hear his baleful call," she said in a sad voice, looking at me with beseeching eyes. I didn't respond and looked straight ahead.

As I was about to back out of the driveway, Sarah hastily got out of the car, saying in a desperate voice, "I can't leave Cam! You can go meet them – tell them I'm sick. But I'm not going."

She walked brusquely towards the house. I sat in the car thinking, "This platypus is changing us in ways I never imagined it would...it seems to rule our lives."

I turned off the car, called my friends and told them the truth: our pet insisted that we stay in. I'm sure they thought us odd, as they have not asked us to go out with them since. Though, really, what do we care?

So, what could we do? We had to still live and function, right? We still had to go to work and socialize with people, because we certainly were not hermits. So, we adjusted.

We decided to get cochlear implants that have recordings of an extensive variety of our platypus's sounds. Also, we purchased digitized contact lenses that allow us to see more than one hundred images of Cam if we blink twice. This way we can go into the outside world, and it appears as if we were engaging with others in work or social settings, but we have our platypus's photos and vocal sounds readily available. Occasionally, or perhaps more than occasionally (haha!), we both miss instructions that people give us at work or things our friends say to us.

Overall, my wife and I continue to be moderately successful both at work and in our social lives. Yet, I must admit, sometimes we get the "Didn't you hear what I just said?" or "Weren't you listening at the meeting when we discussed so and so?"

Honestly, though, this does not faze us in the least. Our platypus has become so integral to our lives that we dread even imagining a world without him...such a world would be truly unlivable.

The Broadcaster

Mickey, a 31-year-old man with red curly hair, had the habit of verbally broadcasting his pre-dream images and dreams to whoever was around. He would broadcast these in a dull, monotone voice as they were occurring.

When he and his wife Danielle, who had raven hair, pale skin and dark brown eyes, started spending nights together about five years ago, she found this tendency of his odd, though a little amusing.

But for the most part, she tuned him out, as his dreams seemed nonsensical. Danielle knew better than to attribute too much to dreams; it would just cause problems over nothing, she felt.

One evening, Mickey was exhausted after having insomnia the previous night. After Mickey returned late from work at 7:30 and ate a quick dinner with Danielle, he went to bed. A few minutes later, Danielle brought her headphones and laptop to bed beside him.

She looked over at him.

Useless. Just useless. Every night he eats dinner and falls right to sleep. Weekends aren't much different. We go to a sports bar and watch a game. If I try to talk, he looks at me like he's annoyed. Why did I marry him? One day goes into the next and they all seem the same. I tried Tawkify and got tons of messages. Maybe I should just go out and meet someone from that. Not to cheat on Mickey, but just to see where it leads. Maybe I'd meet new friends and have more things to do than just sit next to him at sports bars.

Danielle could not help noticing signs of distress on Mickey's face. She paused her show, took out her earbuds and listened.

"Egg eyes, no, eggshell eyes with perforation slits in the middle. Why is that guy running backwards? Where is he going? No, that's stupid. Don't hang from that water slide. The sun's bright, too bright, but that's not the sun, it's a bright color spectrum that keeps changing and has a rip through it, as if it were paper, or maybe paper burning through the center. There's a tension all around, those shoulders look so tense. Am I asleep yet? Just stop focusing on different things. Try a memory. Dinner at Pizzeria Due, Chicago-style pizza in Chicago, with tomato sauce on top and cheese underneath. Danielle's sitting across from me, we're not talking. Have been fighting all day. Eyes of the sun. Sun is blinking, or winking, I can't tell. The sun starts rolling around like a kickball. No, that's not the sun. It's a human head rolling!"

Should I wake him up? Danielle thought.

"There's a train station, but it looks more like a tourist center. It's in Cologne, Germany. I'm traveling with Anthony Ramucci. His face looks like a 9-year-old, but we're all grown up and traveling across Europe. I tell him that I've traveled across Europe before – so I know how things are done. I go up to one of the tourist greeters, who sits behind a high desk, which are lined up along the edges of the circular room. They can't help me. I try another greeter. She can't help and recommends going directly to the train station. She asks, "Does this look like a train station?" I admit that it doesn't. Then Danielle is there, and we trek up an unimaginably steep hill, at almost a 90-degree angle, to the train station. Anthony is gone. We're holding on tight to the side railing. I'm glad that I'm stronger than I was when I visited Europe last time – otherwise, I wouldn't be able to hold on. But what about Danielle? I glance back and see her freefalling in the air, like she's falling out of a building."

Danielle gasped, shook Mickey and said, "Wake up! Wake up!"

Mickey's eyes remained shut.

"The police are jostling me, asking in broken English why I let her fall. I shrug. All I can say is 'I forgot she was behind me.' Danielle's father calls and is incredibly sad. I pretend to act sad and commiserate with him. We talk for a while and then suddenly her father's spirit is lifted when we talk about the Kansas City Chiefs."

Danielle held Mickey's nose, put her lips close to Mickey's left ear and said, "Wake up!"

"The teacher is yelling in my ear. I've fallen asleep again in 11th grade English class. But how have I not graduated high school yet? I'm always so behind! People my age have real jobs, kids and their own families. But I have a college degree – how did I not graduate high school? I'm supposed to give an oral presentation in two days, but I need to avoid it – to call in sick or something. I can't stand in front of the entire class. I have to get away somehow, but I have to graduate from high school...I'm in my thirties for Christ's sake!"

Mickey's eyes flickered open, and he turned toward Danielle, a bit surprised.

"Hey babe. Still awake?" he asked.

"Yep. You ok? You were tossing and turning a lot. Seemed like you had a bad dream."

"Eh, not that bad. Just this recurring dream about not graduating from high school even though I'm 31."

Danielle peered over at him, *I've been with you for five and a half years. And you don't even care if I die, you bastard.*

Mickey stared into the darkness and said, "I also dreamt about how someone I knew died, but it didn't seem to matter. Almost like a weight was released. I know that's wrong to say, but..."

Danielle bit her lower lip, hesitated and said, "Yeah, dreams can be funny like that."

She leapt out of bed and walked out of the room. In the kitchen, she took a steak knife out from an aluminum tray holding utensils.

In less than a minute, she stood over Mickey. Although darkness shrouded her, Mickey noticed both her hands were behind her back.

"Did you get me some water?" Mickey asked.

Water? I'm not your servant!

44

A shimmering object moved through the dark room. Before Mickey could say anything, the sharp kitchen knife pierced deep into his chest. Danielle stabbed him repeatedly until his cries faded away.

She turned on the light and pulled Mickey's dead weight from the bed and onto the floor. She used all her strength to push his body underneath the bed.

After turning out the lights, she lay on the bed and closed her eyes.

For a while she tossed and turned. The room felt so quiet.

Stretching out her hand across the queen bed, Danielle touched a wet spot. She put her hand to her nose, and a metallic smell overwhelmed her, causing her to gag.

Maybe I shouldn't have taken his dreams so seriously, she thought.

A Curious Hospital

A patient had his gastrointestinal system opened. The surgeon realized that there was "too much stuff going on," put her hands up and left the operation room. An hour later another doctor walked in and saw that the patient was fading. The doctor opened the window, wheeled the hospital bed to it and tilted up the bed. The patient slid off and out the window. The dying patient fell on an intern nurse, whose neck snapped.

A senior cardiologist, with dark-rimmed glasses and a graying goatee, walked past the crushed intern. He shook his head, muttering to himself, "Interns." He was joined at the entrance by the hospital's top surgeon, who had a faraway, glassy look in her eyes. They engaged in small talk, such as if the inflatable globes in the children's cancer ward could also be used as kickballs during playtime. Then they discussed the weather, how clouds had gathered, like a metastatic mass, but the sun still shined. Before going to their offices, they placed their hands on each other's genitals, checking for a pulse.

The hospital director showed up in a limo around noon. When the limo driver opened his door, the director, with a light brown, bristle-broom mustache and a bald crown, began practicing a speech he'd deliver to his employees. Approaching the bodies on the walkway, the director paused, and his thin-gloved fingers went to his chin. He nodded and gave the dead patient a quick pat on the back before continuing on his way.

The Tenants

The tenants were selected blindly. The windows were shattered, and dirt was their food.

They warred for Landlord, showing immense fortitude. Sometimes, they'd bring back enemy heads and say, "Here, Landlord, this is enemy." Landlord glanced over and smiled before returning to playing cards with friends.

One time, when Landlord journeyed to Paris for a conference, a few tenants began playing cards, like Landlord. Word spread and the card players were hanged by a tenant mob.

Landlord returned and, again, all was fine and good.

Somehow, a few books fell into the hands of a tenant. The tenant suggested to others that they change the landlord system, that it be based on merit, and for no one to be allowed to suffer. The tenants would have none of this. They tortured and burned her at the stake, shouting with flushed faces, "We like our broken windows! We love to eat dirt!"

Landlord looked over from the card game with a broad smile. He stood up, took off his black top hat, placed it over his chest and said, "I salute you all."

Character and Author

"Whyyyyyy?" a young man says, gazing up to a mountaintop.

Thunder cracks and lightning lights up the overcast afternoon.

"Why am I a white male character?"

The author looks coldly into his half-written manuscript and says, "Because. I am."

"I am who I am because of your dull, unimaginative mind?"

"No, certainly not. This story has a bunch of interesting stuff going on. Just look around you!"

The young man looks around. The forest behind him is bare, bereft of birds and other animals. The mountain is treeless, with scattered large boulders. Thunder and lightning continue.

"But why isn't there any rain coming down? Thunder and lightning and no rain? It seems kind of weird."

"I'll write that in later. I'm on a roll now."

The young man shakes his head, glancing despondently to the ground.

The author rubs his chin and looks at the Word doc.

"If you're unhappy, I can change your sex?"

The young man glares toward the mountaintop.

"Don't look so surprised. I'm open to changing things up."

"You mean I'd get an operation on my you-know-what?"

"Well, I wasn't thinking that, but clearly that's an option. I was thinking more of going back through the manuscript and adding an 's' in front of all the 'he's'."

The young man folds his arms and shakes his head.

"Are you really that lazy? Why am I stuck in the world of such a boorish writer?"

"Hey! That's not fair! Besides, you aren't doing too much yourself. You are the one always getting distracted and complaining."

The young man takes a deep breath, glancing back to the empty forest.

"Sorry...I guess."

"It's ok, it's fine. So, do you want that sex change, either operationally or by me going back and tweaking the manuscript?"

The young man's eyes twinkle defiantly as he looks up towards the mountaintop.

"No! It's too late for that. In the words of Leonard Cohen's *The Butcher*, 'I am what I am.'"

The author chuckles.

"I didn't know that you knew that song!"

"Yup. I sang it to Jessica at the Adirondacks ski lodge in Chapter Four."

The author places his index finger to his lips.

"That was the Stones' *Sweet Virginia*, because the woman's name was actually Virginia."

The young man squints.

"In my recollection it was *The Butcher*."

"Hang on," the author says, scrolling back through the Word document to Chapter Four. He returns to the young man peering up the mountaintop. "Nope, it was definitely *Sweet Virginia*. Jessica was a skier you befriended on the slopes, but weren't interested in."

"Well, whatever. It's a great song. And Jessica was way more my type than Virginia. Virginia eats with her mouth open and never listens when I talk."

"I can't recall you and Virginia ever having a meal together."

"It happened on my own time. Never mind."

"Your own time? There's no such thing!"

The young man bites his lower lip.

"Right."

The two become silent. The author stares blankly into his laptop and the young man looks at the leafless forest.

"So, do you want a sex change?"

"No. I told you; I am what…"

"Ok, I get it. Then maybe you should stop griping about being a white male?"

"I never said that I didn't want to be nonwhite…"

"Yeah? What were you thinking?"

"Colombian, maybe. Or better yet, Filipino."

"Ok. That's not going to be as easy as changing you into a woman, but I can manage."

"Actually, hang on. Wait a second," the young man says, raising his hand like a traffic cop. "I think I'm fine as I am."

"Yeah? Ok, then stop with these empty gestures and the plot can move forward…we need rain, right?"

"Rain would make sense."

"Ok, then I'll give you rain."

Book Reading

My publisher suggested I do a tour southerly, beyond Boston's South Shore foxtail pines, King Phillip's forests along Long Island Sound. He said that there, there'll be bookstore buyers who'll flood the swamp with insecticides and perfumes that will make the heart race.

Along an ocean's edge road, with rocky crags rising up from the sea and sinking back beneath, if one takes a certain back road, between two gigantic hedges, they can reach south Texas. After driving past oceanfront homes on stilts and the loamy crash of waves near San Padres Islands, a reading will be set up at a small bookstore. The rectangular-faced owner with circular eyes and a carrot nose will ask how many people I'll be expecting. Before I can answer, the wind casts her paper body away into the sea. In the empty bookstore, I'm to start reading from my book. Slowly, a few peccaries, a green jay and a spotted ocelot will enter, followed by the outstretched ocean arms.

Latitude or longitude?

Latitude or longitude, that was the question.

The couple was lost in the desiccated Mediterranean salt basin 5.4 million years ago. They built a playground from the wind and a few *Australopithecus afarensis* showed up, although it was before their time.

After the young *A. afarensis* played on the slides and swings, the man held a mirror to their faces and said, "Guess what? Now you're humans."

It was only half-true. Their upper torsos resembled *Homo sapiens,* while their lower halves had devolved into sponges.

The initial question became more urgent as the tectonic plates under the Strait of Gibraltar rumbled and the ocean broke into the western Mediterranean. The woman phoned the Moroccan Coast Guard but was unable to give an exact location other than "near the refilling sea."

The two hugged each other goodbye, gave curt handshakes to the human-sponges and looked toward the thundering flood. The woman tried something that she had once read in a hackneyed, over-quoted book: she held out her arm like a traffic cop and stared, wide-eyed towards the abysmal gray sky, invoking God.

There was a strident clapping sound and hands became visible.

A woman's voice resounded, "Thank you for reading my book. It's not surprising though, since it has been on the best-seller list for millennia. Would you like a signed copy?

The earthly woman's mouth hung open and her husband muttered, "Look," as he gestured towards the flood moving closer on the horizon.

A Moroccan Coast Guard helicopter whirred down, and a rope ladder dropped. From inside, there was a shout imploring the couple to climb up.

As they went up, the woman's voice said, "Don't fly away with these heathens! Accept your fate!"

The couple got into the helicopter as the salt basin below them was inundated. The helicopter moved higher up into the sky and hovered.

A man's deep voice roared from the sky, "They are not heathens. They're people of the book, like you! But this book is newer, with key updates."

"They don't believe in me or my son!"

"You are the unbeliever!"

"Me? I'm God herself. You're the impostor!"

As the helicopter flew away, the couple turned around to see a ghost-like image of a man and a woman arm wrestling.

"They would've loved the playground we built," the earthly woman thought to herself.

Dump

From the early afternoon light filtering through the tavern's off-white shades, Sharon's frown had become apparent. She sat there watching Daryl eat an enormous pulled pork sandwich after finishing her grilled tempeh and arugula salad.

"What?" Daryl asked, taking off his baseball hat and wiping the sweat from his brow.

It was over 90 degrees. From where they sat in the back, not a trickle of air from the doorway fan was palpable.

Sharon's lower jaw sunk low as she started to open her mouth. She placed her pointer finger to her lips and thought for a moment before putting her shoulder-length, red hair into a bun.

"He's not a bro but he's different from me," she thought. "He doesn't get the details of my paintings and how it's only them that matter. Kara even said that the details 'overwhelm and inform' the whole. But the last portrait I did of an old woman, all that Daryl said was, "Very cool." Did he even look at it? I tried to show every skin cell of the woman's face to depict the dark circles around her eyes and all her wrinkles."

"Not talking again?" Daryl asked.

The waiter came by and asked if everything was ok. Sharon responded that all was well, as Daryl had just taken another large bite from his sandwich.

Did they want the check? Sharon shook her head.

It'll be ten years before he finishes that sandwich. He eats so goddamn slow and look how he chews! Like a cow chewing on grass all day. Hurry up, cow!

Sharon tried to remember if Daryl had asked her something. He must've, but what?

"How's your sandwich?"

"It's good."

Sharon raised her eyebrows and nodded.

"Why do you always have to be so sarcastic about everything? You don't have to look down on me for eating meat."

"I don't."

Actually, I do, but not that much. If you just ate chicken and beef occasionally, it'd be different. But you eat beef or pork every day.

Don't you realize how bad that is for the environment? Methane is worse than CO2, dude. And you say you care about climate change. That was probably just to get into my pants.

"I have to say: I'm really loving this conversation we're having."

"Me too."

"See what I mean? And I don't even know if you mean it or not. But I guess not, right? Because we've barely spoken all through lunch."

"That's because you're eating."

"We've both been eating. You're just done."

"Yep, I was done like ten minutes ago."

"Is it a race? I can't help it if this place makes ginormous sandwiches."

"You don't have to eat all of it."

"Come on, this kind of thing would taste horrible the next day. It's eat it all now or waste it, you know?"

"Interesting."

Was he always so boring? He couldn't have been. Or maybe I was just blinded by his good looks and how into me he was.

"Really? You don't find that interesting. You shouldn't say stuff that you don't mean. It almost seems like you're just responding to me on autopilot and you're just way off on another planet or something."

That would be preferable to being with you.

Sharon got up and went to the bathroom. Thick cigarette smoke pervaded the air. The stall she went into had an empty Heineken bottle floating in the toilet.

"Figures," she thought. "He always likes divvy places. Maybe that was cool when you were 21 but not when you're 35!"

When she returned, Daryl was lying on the floor underneath their table, with his head popping out at the end. The plate of pulled pork sandwich, of which there was still one-quarter remaining, was on his stomach. She rested her feet on his ribs as she sat down, and it felt particularly comfortable. The White Stripe song "Stop Breaking Down" came into her head and she tapped out the beat with her heeled shoes.

"I think I got it! That's Green Day's "Basket Case," right?"

"No."

"What is it then?"

"Why does it matter?"

Daryl peered up at her from the floor, trying to make eye contact and asked, "Don't you love me anymore?"

"Did we ever say we loved each other?"

"Yeah, we both did. Remember? We were in Brooklyn at your favorite restaurant in the whole world."

Sharon thought back to a year ago, four months after they had met. They were seated outside at a narrow row of tables next to a dozen-story brick building. It was an Indo-Chinese vegan place. She ordered an amazing Gobi Manchurian appetizer; he just sat there with a coffee, saying that he wasn't hungry. He looked in her eyes and said those words. When she replied in kind, his hazel eyes beamed.

Love is weird. I thought I loved you then, but did I? Maybe? But maybe I was just horny and lonely. I definitely don't love you now.

"Why do we always have to talk about these kinds of things?"

Why do we have to talk at all?

"I don't know. I guess that it's nice to reminisce about the nice times that we've had together."

Sharon looked straight across the table to where Daryl had earlier been sitting and said, "I've been thinking. We've been together for almost a year and a half now. Don't you think it's time to give ourselves a little space and maybe see other people?"

"You mean like an open relationship?"

"No. I just mean us not seeing each other anymore. Ever."

Daryl stopped chewing and looked up at the ceiling fan, which had finally whirred on.

"...I don't think that's something we need to do."

"I do," Sharon said, shoving her heels deep into his side as she pushed herself out from the booth.

She stood up, looked down at him as he masticated on a mouthful of pulled pork and said, "I'm dumping you, Daryl."

Nanny

"Good timing," Giselda thought, taking off her shoes.

Jimmy, the 13-month-old she was hired to watch, had fallen asleep for his morning nap just before she arrived.

Giselda looked out the window, from the dried-up grass on the expansive front lawn to a sign in the neighbor's yard across the street that read "We're proud of our Christian Academy student."

She took out her phone and scrolled through Facebook. Her friend Adriana and her new American husband had posted pictures from a fishing trip to New Hampshire. But Giselda knew that Adriana didn't even like fishing. Giselda's mother had finished reading the Harry Potter series for the fifth time. Her São Paulo high school classmate, Luiz, posted something new against Bolsonaro.

"Would you like a coffee?" asked Lisa, Jimmy's mother, who Giselda had responded to on a local Nannies/Babysitters community page seeking childcare.

"No thank you."

"Good, because I'd have to charge you for it."

Lisa laughed and stood over Giselda, watching her look into her phone.

"How long are his naps, usually?"

"What?" asked Lisa, unaccustomed to ESL speakers.

"Jimmy's naps, are they usually for one hour? Two hours?"

"Oh, I don't know. They could be anywhere from 15 minutes to three hours."

"Wow, quite a range!"

Lisa nodded and walked away.

Giselda fished out a hair tie from her purse and tied her long, silky black hair into a ponytail. She looked at her phone and saw Rodrigo's number pop up. They had broken up two months ago, but he kept calling her to "check on her health." It was around the time that she had Covid when she stopped taking his calls. She had been symptomless for over a month and a half but the only foods she could taste were Guaraná and her roommate's barbeque beef.

Giselda texted, "I'm fine. Stop calling me all the time. Ok?"

A few minutes later, just as she heard fussing coming from Jimmy's upstairs bedroom, Rodrigo texted back, "Ok. But I care about you. If the feeling isn't mutual then I'll just go back to São Paulo."

"No, stay. Not because of me though. I don't think we'll ever get back together. But with the money you make at your fancy job, it doesn't make sense to leave now. Your family needs that."

Rodrigo was a software engineer at a Boston financial firm. Although he didn't make as much as his American colleagues, he was fairly content with his salary.

Giselda felt a tap on her shoulder.

"Umm, excuse me. Did you hear Jimmy?"

Lisa looked down at Giselda with small, squinting blue eyes. Her dirty blonde hair was parted in the middle and tucked behind her ears. When she bent over and tapped Giselda, the right side of her hair fell across half of her face.

"Yes, but it just sounded like a little fussing. Do you want me to go and get him?"

Lisa stood upright and leaned towards the staircase with a tilted head.

"He quieted down. Never mind."

Lisa went back to the kitchen and began chopping vegetables. She turned on the radio to her favorite soft rock station.

"Just as an FYI, I don't pay for the time when he's napping."

"Are you serious?"

"It wouldn't be fair to us. I can't pay you to just sit there. We aren't loaded."

"It doesn't matter if you're loaded or not. This is my time that you have to pay for."

"It's your time to go on Twitter or text your boyfriend. I won't pay for that."

Lisa opened the freezer and took out a plastic bag with several pizza crusts from weeks ago. She placed them into the microwave to defrost, then put them in the toaster until they got warm and crispy and started chewing them while chopping celery.

Giselda remained seated in the family room and stared at the Persian rug. It had multiple gilded borders, each one smaller than the others. In the center, there was a detailed depiction of a king seated on a throne. A woman wearing a wimple clasped his leg with both hands.

"I like that we can still talk," texted Rodrigo.

Giselda started to text back when her phone was snatched away. Lisa stood over Giselda wagging it in her face.

"Hey, we provide free internet service for you here and we aren't a public library. So, drop the sour face, k?"

Giselda gritted her teeth as Lisa handed her phone back. She looked back to the picture of the king and woman. The king had one of his hands on the woman's head, as though he was petting a dog.

Giselda clutched the phone, put her arm back and hurled it at Lisa as she walked away.

"Ouch, fuck!" said Lisa, holding the back of her head where the phone had hit. She pointed towards the door and said, "Get the hell out of my house!"

Giselda walked slowly towards Lisa and picked up her phone from the off-white linoleum kitchen floor.

She caught Lisa's eyes and said, "Gladly, you miserable woman."

The New Employee

With zealous supplication, the techie outlined, at an esteemed presentation, how an algorithm would lift his co-workers off their chairs and carry them to the Exit door, where they would politely be shoved out the door. Two executives at the meeting, who wore angel masks, glanced at each other simultaneously, the corners of their mouths curling upwards.

"And then," the techie continued, encouraged by the executives' responses, "at the side door, which will automatically open, the newest member of our team will walk in. He, she or It, if you like, is a descendant of Deep Blue, who defeated the chess master Garry Kasparov in 1997, as you may recall. This employee is worth its weight in gold."

The techie glanced up to see the executives nodding with approving eyes.

"Does this new employee have a name?" one of the executives inquired.

"Yes, it's Efficiency!" the techie stated with swelling pride.

Almost reflexively, both executives rapidly rose to their feet in applause.

After the clapping subsided, the human resources manager asked, "What if these let-go employees try to get back into the building? Will they still have the code to unlock the door?"

"I'm glad you brought that up," the techie said, with a concerned countenance, his eyes compulsively flitting in the direction of the angel-masked executives. "We are working on coding that will automatically change the lock for the building into the aforementioned algorithm."

"Will this algorithm cover all the loose ends, regarding the soon-to-be former employees' various tasks?" one of the executives asked, with a worried look in his eyes.

"Well, inevitably the algorithm can't cover everything, at least not in the short term. In the meantime, for any loose ends, our vendors in Phnom Penh or Vientiane should be able to handle it."

The techie then asked if there were any questions, to which there were none, and the meeting began to wrap up.

One of the executives glanced out the window that faced a row of picnic tables behind the building where employees were eating lunch.

"Looks like lunchtime!" he exclaimed; a shade of darkness suddenly colored his eyes.

The other executive nodded and told the techie, "I'm really encouraged by your idea. These are very exciting times for the company!"

"I'm just glad to be a part of it!" the techie responded, smiling.

The other executive opened the window facing the lunching employees and, in a deliberate manner, reached under the meeting table and retrieved a high-powered rifle. He then looked through the scope carefully while directing it towards the picnickers and began targeting them, one by one. As cries of agony emerged from outside, the people in the meeting room looked extremely focused on their laptops, as though nothing out of the ordinary was occurring. Only the techie froze, his face suddenly transforming into that of an American foxhound.

When the lunching employees had all fallen or fled, the shooter asked the techie, "Could you please bring up the picnickers?"

The American foxhound-faced techie nodded, "Sure thing!"

As he left out the door, the techie called back to them, "Thanks!"

As dead bodies are weighty and the wounded survivors tried to resist it, the techie took over a half hour to bring about 20-something wounded or dead lunching employees into the meeting room.

When everyone was gathered, the shooter fixed his angel mask, cleared his voice and said in a very earnest tone of voice, "Thank you all for coming. I hope you all had a nice lunch! I just wanted to bring you together to celebrate these exciting times for the company! We've developed a new cutting-edge business methodology, the details of which will be released in the coming weeks. But I'm glad...."

"You bastard!!!" screeched a wounded employee but was immediately silenced after the other executive pointed the rifle at him.

"....as I was saying, I'm glad we are all here together to share this very exciting moment!"

Home, at Last

The backyard is crumbling.

Masked men with machetes butchered the hedges. The pool is a hydrothermal vent where the bacterium LUCA enjoys the floats. Where there isn't dirt, the grass is coarse and tan.

Rabbits have pledged allegiance to a new kind. Squirrels scurry up the trees, hiding forever behind soft, white, flowering leaves. A garden snake slithers over a dirt patch, pauses and stares up at the faded blue sky. Sparrows gawk with dinosaur eyes, though if you look at them, they turn away. Half-faced neighbors peek over the gate and ask how things are.

When my friend comes over, I check her ID.

We talk of peace, love, Russia's invasion of Ukraine and how we don't fund the military nearly enough.

A pregnant woman scales the fence and falls into our dust bowl. After stumbling to her feet, she begs for change. Our tall gate should have prevented this.

We adopt code names for the pregnant woman. "Water" means government handout and "sparrow" is welfare queen.

I say to my friend, "Sparrow wants water but I'm not the water giver. Sparrow has already been given too much water."

The pregnant woman doesn't seem to hear us, but a sparrow stares at us from the top of the fence. The bird's eyes widen as our gazes fixate on it.

The earth suddenly begins to quake. A fault line beneath the yard tears the earth open and we fall in. My friend and I sink downward into the bottomless hole. We finally reach solid ground and are in a new world.

From a clearing, a small band of ruddy-faced, half-clothed hunters pass. We follow them as they look for game. They don't seem to know any language beyond grunts and cries.

At last, we are home.

Polarization

The storm ended our time out. It was a divergence of wills, where we collected sand sculptures and sent them on a huge barge down the Mississippi, slicing the country in half. The sand sculptures depicted our mirrored faces in a frozen state of yell.

During recess, our kickball games were vicious, mocking the other team with unmitigated belligerence. When someone kicked a homerun, in which the ball invariably rolled down the incline of the hot top jungle, and through a tenuous wooded path to a busy street below, an outfielder or two would chase after it. Upon reaching the street, where the red kickball meandered among swerving cars, it was not uncommon to hear yells from drivers like "Get back to where you belong!" In lesser instances, children were driven over, "for the good of the country," as drivers would later tell the police.

Back in class, we had an assignment to write about the seemingly ever-present barge with sand sculptures riding down the Mississippi and why things got like this. One student, Billy, I think his name was, read his answer aloud, "The drip force of the empty refrigerator's precarity and the paycheck's febrile skeleton invariably got people yelling. Instead of shouting at the Pantagruelian foot that walks over them, they chastise each other. Politicians mimic this for theater."

Because Billy spoke in "tongues," as the teacher informed us, he was kept after class and harassed by other students. The next day, he was placed in the outfield, where after chasing a homerun in the nearby street, he was run over.

It's nice that Billy was taught a lesson, the teacher said.

Crusade, or the historic *Other*

In the Acre night, young Palestinian men sat outside shopfronts smoking water pipes and drinking juice. As I walked past them, on narrow streets near the Old City, they may have wondered what kind of crusader I was. Napoleon, with his army, had tried to mount these walls, where six centuries earlier his ancestors had been more successful, albeit only temporarily.

After walking through the Old City, with the late noonday yellow-orange sun casting long shadows out from ancient buildings, I ate chicken shawarma at an outdoor restaurant, where I watched a Palestinian Israeli man fishing with his two boys. As the sun lowered, they left, and a group of friends dared each other on how far out they could climb onto a daunting jetty. I sipped a beer, washing down the shawarma, and was brought back to a Cape Cod jetty, where I'd often urged my younger cousin to act more boldly in the face of the sea's amorphousness.

At a Christmas party back in the States, a family friend greeted me. After we exchanged

"Merry Christmas" to each other, he inquired, "What kind of beer you got there?"

"Effes," I answered.

"Oh, where's that from?" he asked warily.

"It's Turkish," I replied.

He raised his eyebrows in an alarming mien. With a circumspect voice, he said, "Ohhhh...Muslim!?!?!!" before greeting more guests.

--

White-robed Frankish knights, with golden crosses, emblazoned over their chests, pointed towards the Holy Land from their medieval ships sailing the Mediterranean.

From his white-hooded robe, a man's eyes flitted open for just a second; seated in front of a television, he gestured incoherently. From the television, one event came to the forefront and re-played incessantly, until it eclipsed all other news stories. The man seated before the television again closed his eyes, encouraging his fellow knights as they sailed closer to the Holy Land, "We will take care of this problem! We will no longer feel besieged by *them*! This

sacred, stolen land of our savior Jesus Christ –
it will soon be ours!"

Somewhere Else

"It's the same thing in principle," she said, licking her lips and glancing out the bay window that sunlight bathed through, "as me saying 'go fuck yourself'."

He pictured a snake emerging from her squinting, light-green eyes and darting across the room, sinking its fangs into his neck.

The bleeding yellow light beat down on the street, where two pickup trucks had stopped. Two men got out and started chatting with each other. The bearded one wore a long-sleeved Glenwood Cemetery shirt; the other was tall and slender and had a gray fedora on. When the cars behind them beeped for blocking the road, the bearded man shook his head and waved dismissively in their direction.

"Even now, you're not listening to me. We're fighting and you don't care," she said, glancing back towards the window to see what her husband was looking at. As she turned, her black-streaked, dyed-blonde hair trailed her head like a silken Japanese fan.

"They're taking up the road to have a conversation," he said, grinning.

"So what? We're having a conversation too!"

He scratched his thinning curly hair and shrugged. Taking off his glasses, he rubbed his right eye.

"The tent we tried to set up, it was no good – I know. We should've tried setting it up in the backyard before going."

"Is that what you think this is about? A goddamn tent?"

His mouth hung open.

"Isn't that it? You're mad because our overnight got ruined by the leaking tent?"

"Pretty goddamn typical."

He got up and walked to the bay window. The pickup trucks were gone, and the traffic flowed freely.

"Why are you so mad then?"

"That I should even have to answer is reason enough."

"Sorry, I'm not following. I agree. Our trip was ruined by a leak in the…"

"Would you give it up on the fucking tent already? I don't give a shit about that!"

"Ok, ok."

"It's not ok!"

He turned from the window, tilted his head down towards her and their eyes met.

"It's not ok that we've been struggling for the past few months. Actually, more like the past few years, to have any kind of conversation where you're actually *here*. You're always somewhere else, either looking at your phone, playing a stupid video game, watching a football or out somewhere. We haven't sat down and had a conversation for years. I feel like I'm just an object in your eyes. A prop for your friends and family. Someone who's there to serve you chips and beer. I'm telling you, Matthew, I'm tired of being your prop!"

"My prop? That's pretty funny. You've got a job, friends, your own life. I let you do whatever you want, and you do it. If you think of yourself as my prop, it's because you've made yourself one. And, by the way, we talk a lot. Remember that conversation we had last week at Cheesecake Factory about our trip to Nashville last July? I was thinking to myself then, 'Man, we've been together for ten years and still have amazing conversations.'"

"That conversation at Cheesecake lasted exactly one minute and the food came out. And then we talked about that."

"But that's what couples do. They talk about the small stuff!"

"If the depth of conversation we have – after a week of barely talking – is about food, then we have serious problems!"

"I don't think we have problems," he said, sitting back down at the kitchen table and looking sideways towards the window.

Across the street, a short, stout woman with graying brown hair played with her sons, who rode big wheels up and down the driveway. The younger boy fell from his big wheel near the street. He looked back to his mother and waited until she got close before bursting into tears.

She sat down next to Matthew and stared at him.

"Of course, you don't."

Digits

I've been watching you. It isn't weird, it's just the way the color of your hair reflects in the sunlight calls to mind golden, fall leaves, swaying in the wind and wondering when they'll depart from the towering oaks and waft to the ground.

I glance around the room, as though I'm taking in the guests, and steal an extra look in your direction. There is something about your face, with freckles dappling your cheeks, aquiline nose and soft chin. And I think the feeling may be mutual because whenever you look in my direction, you purse your lips and squint, like you're trying not to make it obvious that you're checking me out. Who knows, maybe it's because you sense my hovering eyes and are trying to indicate that it's not wanted.

I'm walking towards you. Why are you trying to balance a wine glass on your head all of the sudden? Are you miming William Tell? Will an imaginary person from across the room try to shoot it off? Or are you trying to impress me?

"Who are you?" you ask, as I join your circle by the window.

Those around you have reacted – the old, bald man with a silver cane frowns, the young woman at your side wears an expectant half-smile and the tall man who looks like he's your sun umbrella seems about to laugh.

I say that I'm no one. A book, a carpet, a wall. You laugh and tilt your head back. The wine glass falls and shatters on the wooden-tiled floor. A look of horror overtakes you, so I start picking up the pieces when the tip of my index finger is ripped open. You get a cloth from the kitchen and press it to my finger.

"It's my fault," you say and offer a ride to the hospital.

You wait with me in the emergency room and outside as they stitch up my finger. At 3:30 in the morning, you drive me home.

I begin to head towards my front door but turn around. You're looking into your phone. Are you texting someone? Your husband?

I tap on the side window.

As you roll it down, I ask, "Can I get your number?"

"Was that your plan all along?"

"Perhaps," I say, smiling as you pen digits onto the back of a mottled business card, before driving off into the dark, honeysuckle morning.

All the Time in the World

A Mickey Mouse chair sits on the front porch, waiting for the next pickup. The elderly man's youngest grandkid just turned 14, so it's time to get rid of it.

"How long has it been out there?" he wonders, looking out at the motorboat in the driveway. "NickNDad" is written in blue, boldface letters across the side. Nick is now 55 and the two haven't been out on the water together in almost two decades.

A young mother with a stroller passes and the man goes out to the front porch.

"Hello there. What a beautiful baby," the old man says, with a wide smile and hands on hips.

"Thank you. Connor say, 'hi' to this nice man."

Connor waves and the man walks down the front steps in his gray, beat-up slippers.

The man bends over and says, "Connor, what a nice name. How old are you?"

"He's almost 20 months."

"Oh, getting up there! I just love babies."

The old man blocks out the sun with one hand and stares at Connor, smiling.

"Have a good day," the woman says, swerving the stroller around the man and walking off.

The man returns inside where he puts on sneakers and a light jacket. He gets in his red pickup truck, which has a hook-shaped bumper sticker of an upside-down fish with its mouth open. The man drives well below the speed limit to a vast, verdant cemetery shrouded in oak and maple.

He kneels at the gravestone of his wife, Helen, blesses himself and whispers a Hail Mary.

Then he sits cross-legged and asks, "How are you this weekend?"

A squirrel runs towards him, pauses a few feet away and chews on an acorn.

"Good to hear. I saw a little baby boy today. He looked exactly like Nick did."

On Helen's gravestone, a jay lands. It twitches its head and flies away.

The man sits in silence for a half hour before standing up and making the sign of the cross.

He begins to walk away, but turns back and says, "Helen, I know that I'll see you soon. You understand why you've had to wait for me all these years?"

A chipmunk scurries through fallen leaves and runs through his legs.

"Yes, the church. But I can't live forever, can I?"

There is a gust of wind. The rustle of fall leaves seems to say, *I have all the time in the world.*

The Romantic

The Romantic finished her ballad and waited for applause. Instead, a child walked to the stage and placed a cup of applesauce at the edge.

The Romantic asked the child, "Aren't you inspired?"

The child shook her head as if shaking off a ravenous swarm of bees.

A parent took the child and said to the singer, "We're inspired!"

The Romantic blushed and 3D-printed a spacecraft from which she launched into orbit. Before long, she was looking down at the earth's oceans and continents.

The singer received a call on the spaceship's bulky, 1990s-style car telephone. It was her manager.

"What are you doing? You're in the middle of a performance!"

"I'm feeling a moment of afflatus."

Eventually the boos from the audience grew so loud that the singer woke up from her spaceship and asked, "How would you all like to hear another song?"

A woman in the front row yelled, "That's what we came here for!"

The singer opened her mouth and inhaled. She closed her eyes and returned to the spaceship. The earth receded into the background, and she sped onwards toward Mars. The weightlessness of the flight overcame her. There was no above or below, just space.

The Romantic sang, "The planets are alive with the sound of music. And it's been that way for five billion years."

When she opened her eyes, the audience was gone. The cup of applesauce on the edge of the stage had a spoon in it, so she sat down cross-legged and ate it up.

Accost

"Even after George Floyd, there was so much opposition, especially from police unions, that efforts to reform the police on a nation-wide level were thwarted," said Anh, a Vietnamese American associate professor with short black hair and black-rimmed glasses.

Someone in the class shouted, "It's 11:30!" Within seconds, the students had filed out of the classroom.

Anh closed *The New Jim Crow* on her desk. Next to the book, her phone lit up.

Davit Borgesian texted her, "Running ten minutes late for Starbucks."

As Anh walked to the Starbucks on the edge of the Philadelphia campus, she hoped Davit wouldn't continue where he had left off the last time that they met. He had been going on about how it took a century for the US to officially recognize the Armenian Genocide as a genocide because Turkey, a NATO ally, would get angry.

"He *is* a Genocide Studies professor," Anh thought, "but did he have to talk about genocide when they drank martinis after work? It wasn't like Jeremy (their other colleague) was interested in hearing a lecture on genocide either."

It was mid-fall, the air cool and crisp, and the sky gray. Dried, orange-maroon leaves raced by Anh's feet as she waited to cross an intersection. The "Walk" sign didn't go on after a bit, so Anh went to press the button but flinched.

An African American boy with a backpack on cried, "Ouch!" and put his pointer finger to his mouth.

"Sorry! Didn't see you there," Anh said. "Are you ok?"

The boy said nothing and walked as far away as he could from her while waiting to cross the street.

When the "Walk" sign went on, Anh walked up to the boy and said, "I'm sorry! I really didn't mean to squish your finger. I hope it doesn't hurt!"

The boy bee-lined for the library, glancing back only after he had climbed up the library steps and had begun to open its heavy front door.

Before she knew it, Anh stood in front of the Starbucks barrister, a chinless white man in his early 20s with a ponytail and a sharp nose.

"What will you be having today?" he asked.

"Pumpkin Spice Latte. Grande."

"Good choice," said the barrister, smiling, before relaying the order to someone hovering behind him.

As she sat on a backless swivel stool at a long counter along the street window, she thought, "Why did I get a Pumpkin Latte? It's just cream and pumpkin spice. Hardly any caffeine!"

There was a nudge at her side. It was Davit.

He sat beside her grinning. He had unkempt curly black hair, boyish puffy cheeks and an aquiline nose. Davit was a little over a foot taller than her, so when he tried to kiss Anh after a holiday party last December, not expecting his sudden movement, Anh moved, and banged her forehead into Davit's chin. He'd had a shiny red bump on his chin for over a week afterwards, which Anh tried to avoid looking at. Davit had not tried anything of the kind since and the two never mentioned the occasion.

"I just had to convince a student that I'm not Muslim," he said, eyeing her for a reaction. "And when that finally worked, I had to convince her that if I was Muslim, that'd be perfectly fine."

Anh raised her eyebrows, shook her head and said, "Honestly, I don't know how some of these kids got into this college."

"Must be sports or something."

"But all our sports teams suck!"

"We're not so bad at hockey."

"Hockey? Are we, really?"

Davit shrugged.

Anh went to the counter to pick up her Pumpkin Spice. When she turned back to go back to her seat, her eyes met Davit's as he walked to the register to give his order. He averted her gaze and fixed his eyes on a ripped-open empty Splenda packet on the floor.

When Anh sat back down, she stirred the top cream into the rest of the latte. She took a large sip and looked out the large glass window.

Suddenly, a black adolescent was sprinting directly at her from outdoors. As he neared the window, he pretended to body slam into her.

Anh fell off her chair and onto the stone floor. The teen keeled over in laughter. His white friend walked up to the window, peered in and slapped his friend five.

Davit was returning with his coffee as he saw this play out. After helping Anh up, he knocked on the window and shouted, gesturing to Anh, "What the fuck? She's hurt!"

Anh wasn't hurt too badly but the teens were still laughing outside, so Davit knocked again on the window and pointed to Anh, who had a few tears coming out of her eyes.

The boys' laughter turned into complete shock. In seconds, the black teen disappeared and reappeared in front of them, inside the Starbucks.

He said, "I'm sorry about that. Didn't mean to get anyone hurt."

"Maybe you didn't mean to, but you did," said Davit.

The boy shrugged and moved towards Davit, stuck out his hand and said, "Look, I'm sorry. What do you want me to say? Let's shake on it."

Davit gritted his teeth as he glanced at Anh's pained eyes. She shrugged.

"We accept your apology," he said, "But I'm not going to shake your hand."

"Why not? Let's shake on it. Make it real!"

"No. We get it, you're sorry, but that doesn't mean we're happy about what happened."

The teen started backing away from them.

"You're not going to shake my hand? What the hell! I said I was sorry."

"I'm not going to play your game just because you're sorry now. You and your friend could hurt someone doing that kind of stuff."

The teen shook his head and started walking away, cursing. Once outside, the two teens began talking and then the white teen pointed to Davit and mouthed, "You're dead," miming a knife slice to the throat.

"Oh man," Davit said. "Now they're pissed off. Nice!"

"Let's just get out of here," said Anh.

Shortly after Davit and Anh left Starbucks, the teens began following them.

One of them shouted, "Look! There's a cop across the street. Tell the cops!"

Anh's silence broke. She turned around and went right up into the teens' faces.

"Look. We're not going to tell the fucking cops. Just leave us alone!"

As Davit and Anh continued walking towards central campus, the teens continued to shout at them, "You're dead" and "Go tell the cops!"

It was nearly a mile away from Starbucks when the teens stopped following them.

"You know what's funny?" asked Anh. "I was just teaching my class *The New Jim Crow*…"

The Piece of Red Hair

A long red hair stretched down from Michael's shoulder to his chest.

Gretchen eyed him as he filled the coffee boiler with water.

"Curious how I make coffee?" he asked.

"No," Gretchen said. She took the hair off his shoulder, held it up before him and asked, "What's this?"

"Looks like a red hair to me."

"Yeah, no kidding. Whose is it?"

"It's from a dream I had…I was walking alone through a dense forest where it was hard to see in front of me and there wasn't much sunlight coming through."

"Sounds like in Connors Woods."

"I think it was, actually…I was walking and spotted a deer eating grass. The deer heard me, looked up and our eyes met. Then it started running right at me. I darted away and before I knew it, I was out of the forest, on a narrow path leading up a hill. I outran the deer but kept turning around to see if it'd emerge from the woods.

In the distance, two women approached. One had long, flowing red hair that glistened under the sun and the other wore a baseball cap that hid her face. I thought to myself, 'I'm going to talk to the one with red hair.'"

"Why are you telling me this?"

"You asked...Anyways, as the women got closer, the one with red hair was actually pretty old, probably in her 70s. The other woman took off her baseball hat and had the same long red hair going down her shoulders. They must've been mother and daughter. The daughter had pale skin, full red lips and forest-green eyes that matched the trees. I stopped walking just to look at her."

"Oh, Jesus."

"Right. And that's exactly when you came running out of the woods! As the deer came closer, it turned into you, but it was the teenage you with a nose ring and that haircut you used to have, with two long thick strands of pink hair in the front and the rest of your head shaved."

"I remember that. Guys in high school used to ask, 'Why did you shave your head? Don't you want to look like a girl?'"

"What did you say back?"

"Nothing. I just stared at them like I was going to bury them alive."

"I know that stare! But that's not what you were doing when you saw us. You started pulling at the young woman's hair. She didn't seem to mind, oddly enough. She just looked at her mother with an eye roll, as if this were the kind of inconvenience that she always faced. It was one of the risks, I guess, of being a knockout. By the time you were done with the younger woman, you had pulled out half of her hair. The mother tried to pull out her own hair so she could give some to her daughter. I felt bad for the daughter, so I tried to kiss her, but you put your hand between our mouths. Then you pushed me back and spit at me. You yelled something that I couldn't understand and threw a clump of her red hair at me, which landed right on my shoulder."

Gretchen smiled, shook her head and held up the long piece of hair.

"So, that's where this came from? You bastard!"

Deletion

"What's happening?" asked Sheryl Marley.

"Sorry, it's just not working anymore," Mary Kelly said, peering into her laptop.

"But I'm interesting!"

Sheryl glanced out from the laptop, took a pocketknife from her jeans pocket and rolled up her right sleeve. She pressed down on the blade and ran it across her forearm. Blood oozed out.

"See?"

"That's just a flesh wound. It'll heal in no time. And there's nothing in the story that would drive you to do that."

"We can make something up. Let's brainstorm!"

Mary went to her office window. A postwoman had opened the mailbox and left a few envelopes inside. Mary raced outside and brought in the mail.

"Just as I thought," she muttered, sitting back at her laptop and glancing at a piece of mail from Sheryl, with the return address: "City Library, Midwest, USA 12345."

"How'd you pull that off?" Mary asked.

"What?"

"You know what: sending me mail."

"I have my ways."

"That's strange. It just shouldn't happen."

"Did you open it?"

Mary looked down at the envelope and hesitated. She thought back to the time Sheryl went into a post office in Chapter Four. It was first written as a botched robbery that Sheryl witnessed. Mary changed the scene but never had the chance to clean it up. During the chaos, Sheryl must've conned a postal worker into sending a special kind of mail.

Mary opened the envelope. The header read:

"WARNING!!! YOU WILL BE EVICTED FROM YOUR HOME IF"

Followed by, "you stop working on the beautifully written story of Sheryl Marley's search for meaning and love."

"Search for meaning? Really?" Mary asked, scrolling through the story.

"Yeah, I know you didn't add that part yet, but I thought it would be a nice touch."

"It doesn't have to be about meaning. You could change me into a naughty schoolgirl-type who hasn't grown up yet…That would be fun."

"For whom? You? You're a quiet bookworm-type who's always in the library reading medieval literature. You love *Gargantua and Pantagruel* – you're not the 'fun' type."

"I just don't know if that's who I really am."

"You're exactly who I say you are."

"Who reads medieval literature? I don't want to be a bore!"

"Well, it goes with the character."

"Not if I have any say in it!"

"That's the thing, you don't!"

"Isn't that authoritarian? I didn't think you were that person."

"I can't control anything else in my life, at least I can control you!"

Sheryl closed her eyes. Facing upward, she put up her hands, miming being handcuffed.

"Fine, take me!"

"I'll do exactly that!"

Mary highlighted the entire story and pounded 'Delete'.

flushing bullshit

If you've ever heard of the phrase 'turnaround', then you'd understand that the thickness of yarn reflects the temerity of intestines: how much guts do you have? Guts are the area of the stomach, deluged with microbial wands, that break down food from its already post-masticatory state. It is where the bullshit that gets past the mouth, teeth and tongue is further tattered to shreds, allowing the food's individual components to become visible. And what do these individual components do? Typically, they go to the organs and bones through intercellular transport, fueling one for the rest of the day. And the same thing recurs in a vat of timelessness.

However, if – and this is a big if – one allows the retina to follow its natural inclination to track post-mastication food down the esophagus and into the gastrointestinal system, with a flashlight in tow, then one can see how the guts break down food. Then, before automatically sending proteins and vitamins to organs and bones, the bullshit is placed in a boxcar that rides both to the anus and genitals, where it is released.

When bullshit is pissed or shat, the results are breathtaking.

Picture an Amalfi coast morning, comfortable temperature, feet in the pearly blue Mediterranean, high mountain peaks above and Salerno in the distance. It is really that good. It is then just you and the ocean, not the bullshit stress of a scurrying worker running eagerly to boss, not worries of the weatherman's wolf-fanged snowstorm, not the paranoia that a terrorist will blow you up, not worn down by political media telling you to run this way and that, suggesting you think in the framework they dictate.

No, it is just you and the sea riding a boat to Salerno.

The bullshit captain claims passengers do not know the way themselves, that only he and a pink-haired robot at the helm can accurately guide the ship. When the captain tries to scare passengers of Salerno muggers and sea monsters, he is promptly thrown overboard.

Salerno becomes closer, but it's not a destination, just a stopping place for you and the sea.

Soon after the captain is ousted, the pink-haired robot, wearing Dr Pangloss's glasses, cheers, "We didn't really need a human captain anyways, you have me! Throwing him off is all for the best!"

Abruptly, the robot is also thrown over.

Jesus's Bloody Nose

God flicked an eyelash off his cheek. One of his sons was missing.

He was twirling a baton at a college football game. The band played a Panthers' fight song as the ball was on the 15-yard line.

"Jesus Christ," God muttered upon finding him.

Jesus looked around. The baton, spiraling in mid-air, came down and hit him in the nose. Blood gushed out and a few cheerleaders helped him to the locker room.

Meanwhile, the Panthers slowly edged closer to the end zone. The crowd and even God were at the edge of their seats.

In the locker room, Jesus's nose stopped bleeding and a cotton ball was placed in his left nostril. He lay on the locker room bench, staring up at the gray ceiling, thinking, "Where are you now, God?"

God had descended from up on high and took the form of a business tycoon. He sat in a glassed-in, upper-level box seat and had a set of binoculars to get an optimal view of the football game. Sipping on a neat bourbon, he wore a ten-gallon hat and spoke with a mix of Texan and Australian accents to the waiter.

A half-hour later, Jesus emerged from the locker room. He sat by the cheerleaders but didn't get involved in cheering. It wasn't long before Jesus spotted God; God's curly handlebar mustache gave him away.

"That bastard," Jesus muttered.

God looked down towards Jesus and the earth quaked. Hundreds of lepers surrounded Jesus, begging, and everyone else in the stadium vanished. Swarms of bees and mosquitos hovered around Jesus's head and a Viking ran at Jesus swinging an ax.

"Repent!" God shouted through a megaphone.

Seeing the ax's blade near his neck, Jesus said, "Ok! I repent!"

The insect swarm, the Viking's ax and lepers disappeared, and the Panthers' game resumed.

In the box seat above, Jesus saw God look to him, raise his neat bourbon glass, eyes twinkling like Van Gogh's *Starry Night*.

Terrorism Begins at Home

If you live in New England, early September often has mornings with a chill in the air, where the sun wakes up late, dew floods the grass and, above, the cloudless azure mirrors eternity. As the sun moves higher up in the sky, with the desiccated summer heat gone, a perfect California-type of air takes over. Leaves have not yet turned orange, red or brown, nor have they fallen from their branches. Many people still wear their shorts and tee shirts from mid-summer.

September 11, 2001, was one of those mornings.

I was with a crew building a deck in Derry, New Hampshire when I received the phone call. Only the footings, beams and support posts were built. I was underneath the beams, starting to hammer the joists into place.

It was my uncle, so I picked up the call.

"It's over," he said, sniffling.

"What are you talking about?"

"Aaron was in the towers. He worked on the 34th floor. I tried calling but he's not picking up."

"I wouldn't worry about it. He probably went out for a coffee."

"You're not listening, Mike! He was in the towers!"

"So?" I asked.

The other line went dead.

I continued working and a short while later, Jose said, "Holy shit! Planes hit the World Trade Center in New York!"

And you know the story.

First, there was confusion: which towers were hit, which fell, which might fall, were there still hijacked planes haunting American skies, how many people died and who did this. Amidst these questions, complete shock set in while watching reruns of planes flying into the towers.

As the days went by, shock and confusion turned into anger and rage seething like a rabid dog foaming at the mouth.

That was my first fall after high school. I didn't have a lot happening other than building decks and going to rock clubs around Boston with a fake ID. I had a good friend who was a 'truther' before that became a thing. In less than two weeks after the attacks, he was already relaying to me conspiracy theories about September 11th that he read on the internet. But I didn't buy them.

As it became colder and hammering nails into nascent decks continued, I felt myself changing.

The deck crew debated whether we should attack Afghanistan, Iraq or even bomb the entire Middle East, besides Israel. But I didn't get involved. I just focused on hammering, as if studying the repeat of metal going into wood would bury what was bothering me.

I began to realize that there were enemies among us. And when I say 'us' I don't mean white people, black people, or any group in particular; I just mean there was a feeling that anyone could be a terrorist, even the people I worked with. They may have talked a good game about wanting to bomb the Middle East. But what if that was just a front? How could I be sure that one of them wouldn't bomb my family's house?

In late October we were at a job in Brattleboro, Vermont. It was pouring out. The rain came down in sheet metal with golf ball-sized sleet mixed in. For some reason, the other guys in the crew didn't seem to mind. They went about their work like it was any other day and, as usual, talked politics and what the US should do in response to 9/11.

The crew leader, Jerry, turned to me and said, "Mike, we never hear from you. What do you think we should do?"

I stopped hammering and looked at him. He had a wide, puffy face, short, dirty blonde hair and was smiling. His face was soaking, and he'd occasionally wipe his brow with a towel that we used to remove deck stain from our hands.

"It doesn't matter what I think."

"Why not?"

"Because I'm not the government."

He and the other three in the crew laughed.

"Thank God for that!"

"You're missing the point," I said.

"Oh yeah? And what's that?"

"Terrorists could be anyone. You, Roy, Joe, Jose. Anyone. I could be a terrorist."

"Whoa…Easy there, kid. This is just a laidback conversation…"

They left me alone after that.

There were other disturbing news stories of an attempted shoe bomb on an airplane, anthrax was mailed to congresspeople and there was always an 'orange' – High – alert for a possible terrorist attack. Anything could happen at any moment. I tried to explain this to my conspiracy theorist friend, but he insisted that was just the narrative we were "fed."

One night this friend and I went to Jackie's Diner, a bar with a small restaurant downstairs and a dim room upstairs where local rock bands performed. That night Drowned Thought Machine was playing. The singer had a foot-high blonde mohawk, clear, light blue eyes and tattoos all over his arms and neck. When he sang, he tried to catch each of the audience members' eyes. The bass player was a lanky woman over six-feet tall with an expressionless face. The guitarist had a black-haired mohawk, dark-rimmed glasses and chain-smoked cigarettes throughout the set. The drummer in the back was barely visible and she sang backup vocals to a few songs.

Like a lot of bands that we saw in those days, the music was a mix of hard rock, blues and punk – the kind that the White Stripes would soon popularize. Although my friend and I weren't dancing like most of the crowd, we stood right in front. It was loud as hell, and I knew my ears would ring the next day.

Towards the end of the set, a song began with a catchy, thudding, John Bonham-style beat on the drums. The guitarist was trying to light another cigarette, but the lighter didn't work, and the bassist was at the bar getting a drink. The singer looked wide-eyed at the audience like he was possessed. He half-sang, half-shouted the same lyrics over and over. At first, I couldn't make out what he was saying. People in the crowd started eyeing one another. Soon, it became clear that he was shouting, "Making bombs for the Taliban! I'm making bombs for the Taliban!" After a few minutes, the guitarist and bassist accompanied the music, but the lyrics didn't change at all during the seven-minute song.

The singer proved my theory: terrorists could be anyone. They could be you. They could be me. One thing was for sure: the singer was one of them. In retrospect, some might say the lyrics were ironic or that he was critiquing US policy towards Afghanistan. But I could see in his frenzied eyes that he was making bombs to be used on American households. If I didn't do something, he might blow up my family's house.

116

I went to the bathroom with a glass in hand and broke the top off on the porcelain sink. Its jagged edges gleamed under the bright bathroom lights like a jaguar's fangs. I stuffed it into my flannel shirt, went back to the performance and stood beside my friend. When the song ended, I walked up to the singer.

His eyes had become less frenzied. He smiled at me and probably thought I was going to compliment the music.

"Hey, man. What's up?" he asked.

I shrugged and turned back to the audience, who all seemed to egg me on.

I turned back to him. His mouth was open, and he was about to say something.

I reached under my shirt and removed the jagged glass. Holding the flat end, I jabbed the toothed end deep into his neck several times before being pulled away by the audience.

Today is another one of those early September mornings. The air is chilly and the sky bluer than the sea. A light breeze runs through my fingers as I walk out of prison on the 20th anniversary of 9/11.

A few weeks ago, the Taliban retook Afghanistan.

But you can be sure that the Nazi-lookalike singer with the blonde mohawk won't be making bombs for them this time.

Lottery

In the 40th week, he rose through a filmy, thick fluid, took a right turn at the skating rink and continued to 7-11. He wanted a super-sized Slushie that evolution goaded him towards with pulsating lights and imploding tunnels. At the 7-11 parking lot, he slipped and lay on a sullen gray curbstone.

A woman whose nametag was 'Heather,' with ethereal eyes and flooded hair picked him up, kissed his bare head and, after entering 7-11, told the clerk, "I'll take this infant and a pack of Marlboro Lights."

The clerk asked if she wanted to play the lottery and unbutton the future's vaporous mirror. She shook her head, "I know what's going to happen."

The clerk looked in Heather's swirling yellow-purple eyes and said silently, "You're missing out."

Heather shrugged, took the newborn into her arms and left the store.

Upon emerging, blue thunder sledgehammered the sky and a heavy monsoon fell. From a nearby hill, a surging flood headed towards Heather and the baby. As it reached them, Heather found herself on a surfboard, riding a wave, huddled close to the newborn.

Three years later Heather opened her eyes and found herself on a deserted island. She walked past the glowing beach sand into a forest of cinnamon ferns and high Eastern white pines. After traversing the woods, she was back inside 7-11 where the clerk looked at her with a mischievous grin.

"I'll try the lottery this time," Heather said.

Alarm clock

I've run in circles to mend the harvest. Grain crops have wilted. God told the sun to bend its head on grain and never let up.

I don't blame God for the drought, not directly anyways, but I did tell grain that it ain't on me.

A few farmers in the area say that the climate has changed because of humans. They don't know their foot from their arsehole. I told them, of course, the climate has changed. It changes every year – don't you notice that it's never the same? And, anyways, if it was caused by us, then why don't we just change it back to how it was? This caused them to give me a funny stare, with confused eyes and their jaws dropping low. They were probably thinking, "My God, why hasn't anyone ever pointed this out before?" or maybe "That guy is smart; he got me. Now I have to think of a comeback." They usually just end up either shaking their head or saying something like, "It's not that simple."

I don't think God is evil to cause the drought. I just think that these past couple of years He's been taking a long nap, letting fires rage across California and New Mexico, wild floods deluge Germany and causing no rainfall here.

I'm not sure if God has a wife or not, but someone needs to buy that boy an alarm clock.

Fomorians

You're a piss reminder of an everlasting hotel.

She spoke in a fiery tone. The man waddled side-to-side and began patting a penguin.

He glanced at a chalkboard behind the penguin, where were written the words:

We've broken
glass, crushed
marigold eyes,
dethroned
coughing
cathedrals,
driven Zambonis
over
subterranean
rinks, planted
flowers that
scratch out
esophagi – and
now this?

But he just patted the penguin, holding his tongue.

The day was one of God's many lambs that would 'accidentally' be allowed to wander from the flock and get ripped apart by wolves.

Their house was a homeless person's castle, where they'd sleep on ceilings, break bread with hammers and cook up Bengali fritters for guests. The passerby would never imagine: behind quiet townhouse walls, Cerberus wandered amidst two Fomorians.

She lambasted the cells far beneath his skin. He held his tongue, patted the penguin and read the chalkboard behind the bird. Often, the board's words were illegible, causing him to grit his teeth so hard that the veins on his forehead swelled up like glowing purple rivers.

Eventually she began to tire. Then he shot her with a stabbing glare. Unlike her impassioned rage, his brief words were an ice-cold, tightly sealed box of highly enriched uranium that destroyed villages and maimed metropolises.

When he finished, they traded a few last barbs before flying off to separate rooms.

The house was in shellshock. Befuddled cats twitched, pupils dilated, looking up to the Fomorians in panic. Books and magazines lay scattered across the floor. Blood-red tomato juice stained the wall, leading to the half-splattered fruit on the floor.

On the radio, Orson Welles warned of the high potential for aftershock, should the devolved Hansel and Gretel meet near a hungry witch's oven.

The Real United States[1]

We became free from the Fake US soon after Clarence Thomas died in late 2022 and Election-Steal President Joe Biden appointed Aisha Johnson, an affirmative action hire, to take Thomas's place. That gave the communists control of the Supreme Court, with traitor John Roberts leading the pack.

With all three branches of government under socialist domination, we in the South, Midwest and most of the north-central mountain West, like Montana and Wyoming, seceded and created the Real United States. This didn't start a civil war but there were skirmishes in what the liberal media calls "purple states," like Michigan, Pennsylvania and Arizona. Most of these traitorous states ended up remaining part of the Fake US because they were too chickenshit to be free.

We didn't bother to have an election once we became free. Our leader, my friend, was crystal clear.

---

[1] This story contains offensive content and is written for satiric effect.

But tragedy hit us early on. Delivering the 'State of the Real' address while recovering from a second bout of the fake virus, He passed out. He soon fell into a coma and died 32 days later. Then Vice President Rudy Giuliani was sworn in.

Three days on, a live broadcast showed our leader rising up through the blue sky. During ascent, He waved goodbye to all of us. When He turned back towards the sky, continuing His rise, a cloud changed shape and became Jesus, who walked with him, hand-in-hand, to the promised land in the deep beyond.

He has been canonized and is now considered an equal with Christ and the Holy Ghost. There's even a popular offshoot movement in Idaho and Montana that has taken Jesus out of Christianity and substituted our Leader in. I disagree with them because those people claim that Christ was a Jew, which obviously couldn't be true, because the man started Christianity after all.

I must admit that Giuliani is a little too ethnic for our taste. Frankly, he looks a little too much like a vampire to be a real president. But he is a true warrior. The Second Stage Council, made up of Josh Hawley, Ted Cruz, Tucker Carlson and Sean Hannity, is currently trying to determine who our Leader's true successor will be.

We have several militias instead of a police force or standing army. While they repel threats from the Fake US and from the Mexican rapists to the south, they don't have an organized structure. The Oath Keepers, Three Percenters, Proud Boys and Bundy militias regularly patrol neighborhoods and national borders with automatic weapons and occasionally stop into houses to collect protection dues. Because, after all, this is a free country, and you get what you pay for.

My neighbor was skeptical about this sort of system, although he was committed to our Leader. So, when the Three Percenters stopped by his house to collect, he refused to pay, insisting that militia should be absorbed into a formal police and military force. They took him and shot him dead outside his house. And wouldn't you know – the fake media in the commie north claimed that this was "another racist attack" in our country.

But they are dead wrong, my friend. My neighbor was extremely popular with others. I didn't even know he was black until I later learned, from nationwide mandatory genetic testing, that he was only two-fifths white. But I don't think that's why they hung him. There are plenty of African Americans in the Real USA who live happy, fulfilling lives, and they're treated like everyone else. If they pay their dues and never get into any debt, they have the full respect of the community and militias. If they don't, like others, they become pariahs. Because that's how it is in our free country. You get what you pay for.

Ghost Writer

The soap holder on the shower's lower right-hand side was once sheen black. After years of neglect, it had become ray from a thick film of soap scum.

When the prominent labor rights advocate Albert Wilbur sat on his toilet, he often looked at the soap holder. There was a small object on it that was unidentifiable. He figured that if he or his wife ever did a deep clean of the shower, they would remove the soap holder item and dispose of it. Albert sometimes considered cleaning the soap holder after flushing the toilet, but with all the bacteria accumulated on it, that would require a great deal of time.

He was sitting on the toilet one morning, before beginning a day's work. On his Kindle, a *Guardian* story described how teachers across the US were striking for better pay, more funding for classroom materials and benefit increases. An old Edison lightbulb illuminated in his mind. He came up with an idea for a *Washington Post* op-ed. It would compare teachers' salaries with other well-regarded positions and highlight how teachers' pay dwarfs in comparison. Albert cut his bathroom hour short and walked swiftly across several rooms of his family's stately upper-middle class home to his second-floor office, which overlooked a small manmade pond.

"Jessica," he started an email, "can you write an op-ed for me? It would argue that teachers deserve a raise because they are paid far less than other professions."

Sent.

"Oh shit," Albert muttered to himself, getting up from his chair and walking back to the bathroom. Once inside, he sat down on the toilet and out came the world.

"Uhhhhhh…no," Albert thought, "I should've had more rice with that chicken vindaloo!"

Glancing to his right, he focused on the shower soap holder's small, unknown object.

The morning sun had risen, shooting sharp beams of light into his eyes. Albert fished around in his pocket for his phone, but it was empty except for his wallet. He heard footsteps coming up the stairs.

"I'm taking off, Hunny. Have a good day!" His wife Margaret said.

Albert did not answer, thinking, "She'll think I can't hear her."

Margaret walked up a couple more steps and let out a loud sniffing sound. For a second, she lingered on the stairway.

"What the hell is she doing? Just leave!" Albert thought.

"You ok, Hunny?"

"Yeah, I'm fine! Aren't you going to go to work?"

"I'm going. Don't get snippy with me. Just seeing if you're ok."

"I'm doing fine!"

"You don't sound it!"

Albert listened closely to Margaret's car door open and shut, and to the hybrid Ford roll away down the driveway.

A drop of sweat fell onto Albert's hand.

"Am I coming down with a fever?" he wondered. "It seems like everyone's getting sick now. Or maybe it's the heat that's turned up too high."

"Albert!" a woman's voice called from a distance.

"What is it now?"

"Nothing!" said the voice, followed by a chuckle.

The voice had a thin velvety nature. The more Albert thought about it, he was not sure if it was Margaret or Jessica, as they had similar voices.

Another burst of diarrhea flooded into the toilet.

"Jesus," Albert muttered.

"But Jesus was not a good writer!" said the voice in a quiet tone that seemed to emanate from inside the bathroom.

Albert peered intently at the small object on the shower soap holder. Whatever the object was, it seemed to be moving slightly; although, it was hard to determine if it was even moving at all. Albert continued to stare at the object, trying to figure out if it moved when he heard the woman's voice.

He flinched when he heard a loud scratching sound coming from the door. Seeing the shadow of a small animal, he realized that it was his cat, Furry, and he lent over, opening the door to let him in. Furry was a black mass of hair, to the extent that Furry's eyes, mouth and nose were barely visible.

The cat rubbed up against Albert's legs and he gave Furry a scratch behind the ears.

"A cat could probably write better than you," said the velvety voice.

Albert laughed, then squeezed his lower lip between his thumb and pointer finger.

"Jessica?"

Furry meowed and Albert responded with a few quick pats.

"Margaret?" asked Albert.

He remembered the soap holder, looked to his right, and became determined not to take his eyes away from it.

Furry meowed again, looking towards the bathroom door and back to Albert.

"Ok," said Albert, opening the door and Furry scurried away.

Albert began wiping his ass, which took a while.

"Albert, you dirty son of a bitch! You can't handle Indian food, can you?"

Albert shrugged and stared at the soap holder.

Certainly, there was an object moving on it. He leaned over from the toilet, resting his right hand on the shower's edge to get a closer look. The mysterious object was the plastic cover of a shaving razor head, which seemed to be walking slowly forward to the edge of the soap holder, then to the back of it, and forward again.

"Hello, Albert!" the woman's voice said, "How does it feel to look into my eyes!"

"You have no eyes."

"But I have eyes to see the world, unlike you. You only have one thought and then I say all the rest."

"Jessica? Is that you? But how are you talking to me?"

"It's not me. There is no me. Just you. It's all you!"

"That's silly! I have a lot of respect for you, Jessica…if that is you."

"I'm not Jessica, but if I were, that would mean a lot coming from you – you, who give great interviews about labor rights but cannot stitch together one sentence worth publishing!"

"That's not fair! I have no time. I need good people like you, who I trust, to write good pieces for me."

Albert waited for a response, but after five minutes, none came. He continued wiping his ass, then flushed the toilet, washed his hands and threw water on his face.

"Wow, that was quite a shit," he thought, flushed the toilet again and glanced back at the shower soap holder, which was now empty. He bent over to observe it meticulously. There was nothing but a thick film of white soap scum.

He shook his head and returned to his office, where he sat down and opened his email. There was no response from Jessica.

Albert's phone rang.

Jessica said, "Hi, Mr. Wilbur."

"Hello, Jessica. How are you?"

"I'm well."

A silence enveloped the call.

Albert cleared his voice and asked, "How may I help you?"

"I had a question I wanted to ask you, Mr. Wilbur."

"Ok. What is it?"

"Have you ever seen the show *The Office*?"

"Yeah, but not for a while. Why do you ask?"

"Do you remember that guy Stanley, the salesman?"

"Uhhh…yeah, I think I do."

"Well, in the words of Stanley: you should go on and take a glass of Gatorade, drink it quickly and eat a dry piece of toast. Then you can take all my op-eds that I've written for you and shove them up your butt!"

The Special Suite

The off-white marble ceiling looked down on the couple and their child as they entered the hotel lobby. Behind the concierge desk, a man with long brown hair, glasses, and sideburns that were disconnected from his beard and mustache, smiled at them. A blonde-haired woman trainee with a child-like face stood next to him, watching as he typed onto a desktop computer.

"Hi, we have a reservation," said Rekha, who was tall and had black hair flowing out from underneath her wool hat.

"Certainly, what's the name?" the male concierge asked.

"Mukherjee-Reed."

"You're staying for two nights?"

"Yeah."

"Great, your room is 345. Breakfast will be served from seven until ten and coffee is available all day."

Rekha and her husband, Brad, and their 8-month-old, Hudson, started for the elevator.

The male concierge said, "Oh, I forgot to mention one thing."

"What's that?" Brad asked.

"There've been some complaints about bird sounds coming from the vent around sunrise. But those people were on the other side of the hotel from where you'll be staying."

Rekha yawned and said, "Well, I guess a natural alarm clock then."

"Yeah, exactly. But you won't be affected by it. Have a good evening."

They took the elevator up to the third floor, where a thick, whitish dust pervaded the air. Once in the room, Rekha and Brad laid down on their king bed and closed their eyes. Hudson remained sleeping in the stroller.

The drive from Charlotte to Richmond had been challenging. The trip was normally not more than four hours, but they got stuck in an hour's worth of morning rush hour traffic leaving Charlotte. Near the state line, Hudson cried. They pulled over at a rest area to feed him and change his diaper. It was 2:30 when they went back onto the highway, and they hit afternoon rush hour traffic outside of

Richmond. Hudson started screaming, not wanting to be confined to a car seat any longer.

By 4:30, they had finally reached the hotel.

They were asleep for less than 15 minutes when a banging noise came from the next room.

Brad opened his right eye and thought, "They must be having sex."

Hudson and Rekha were still sleeping, and the sound went away. Brad shut his eyes and fell back into dreamland.

Ten minutes later, the entire room shook, and the loud banging sound returned.

"What is that?" asked Rekha, sitting up in bed.

Hudson began crying. Brad carried him out of the carriage and walked over to the window. All that was visible in the darkness were the closed shades of other hotel rooms, with yellow light glowing out from the window's edges. In the distance, a few skyscrapers overlooked the hotel.

"Construction, I guess. But what a weird time for it."

Rekha left their room to investigate and, sure enough, the room next to theirs was gutted. Two men were drilling panels into the wall.

She went down to the front desk and said to the woman concierge, "There's construction in the room next to us."

"I'll get my trainer."

In a few minutes, the male concierge emerged. He tilted his head to the side and asked, "How may I be of service?"

Rekha repeated what she had told the woman.

"It's not quite five yet, still part of the workday. And, depending on who you are, some people work until six."

"But this is a hotel...I'd like a room change."

"Oh? Are the birds bothering you? Maybe they're constructing a nest. In that case, it's just nature, and I don't think there's much we can do."

"We'll leave this hotel right now and demand a full refund unless you change our room. And we'll give this place a horrible review."

The concierge muttered to the trainee, "Apparently, some people don't appreciate nature...do you happen to see any other rooms available?"

"Not that I can see."

The man leaned over, looked at her desktop computer and asked, "What about up there? They won't hear birds building their nests in the vents there. Plus, it's close to nature."

Rekha said, "We don't want to be close to nature. We just want a quiet room where we can relax."

"Of course, you do," said the man, "and we completely understand that. I think you'll be happy in our new, special suite. It has the charm of the old with a flare of the new. It's close to nature, while being extremely quiet. We think you'll love it."

He handed Rekha an old-fashioned key.

"Just go up to the fourth floor and it's the last door in the hall. There are a few stairs to go up...I really can't wait to hear what you think."

The family packed their luggage and took the elevator up to the next floor. Rekha and Brad exchanged glances as the lights at the end of the hallway dimmed.

They unlocked a door that led to a brightly lit stairway, which had Max Ernst replicas decorating the walls. Rekha took Hudson out of the carriage and carried him, Brad took the luggage, and they trudged up the stairs.

At the top, Brad placed the luggage down and after some difficulty, jiggled the key into the lock. The knob turned but the door was stuck. They both pushed on the door, Rekha with her back and Brad with his shoulder, until it finally squeaked open.

They stepped out into a gust of bitter cold February wind as the door slammed shut behind them. The Richmond skyline was before them with snow flurries falling.

An unknown number showed up on Rekha's cellphone.

When she answered, a familiar male voice asked, "How do you like our new special suite?"

Chicken Bone

My neighbor's dog, Ginger, died from eating a chicken bone.

We were driving home and stopped at a red light when my parents told me. A few weeks later, Ginger's owner also died. I wasn't told how but I presumed it was also from a chicken bone, as I was informed of the news at the same intersection. Each time, the smell of McDonald's oily, fried food bleated through the glass windows. My parents said that they'd be attending his funeral without me because I was too young. I figured that the church for the funeral was exclusively for people closer in age to death. I didn't want to sit through a long mass with a corpse up at the front, anyways.

Twenty years later, I stayed in Florence, or Firenze as the Italians say, for some time. After a few weeks, the friends I traveled with became tired of Italian food, so we began going to a Pakistani restaurant in Santo Spirito, away from the tourists.

An oily, intense curry chicken and rice were gorged on. Beer glasses were emptied quicker than drought grass imbibes rain. One of the pieces of chicken that I bit into had a bone in it, which I didn't realize until it broke into several pieces in my mouth. Not wanting to spit out its contents at the busy restaurant, I was determined to chew the broken pieces of bone up and eat it, even if it meant going the way of Ginger and his owner.

As I chewed, my friends were debating whether we should try to learn Italian. My girlfriend thought it was a good idea in order to blend in, but my two male friends didn't agree because we'd be leaving in a couple of weeks, and we'd rarely use the language upon getting home.

Meanwhile, my mind shifted to the church where Ginger's owner was laid to rest.

I walked down the center aisle of the crowded church where I had attended mass several times as a child. It had enormous stained-glass windows along the side walls and an enormous casket at the front. The priest announced he would deliver a reading from the *Book of Corinthians*. Although I was curious to see what the man who I once knew looked like, a turtle shell had wrapped itself around my body, slowing me down. As I neared the front of the church, my parents sat in one of the pews with a small, white-and-tan dog on their lap. The dog was gnawing on a bone but stopped to look up at me. Ginger's light blue eyes shone under the high church lights.

The priest's voice thundered, "For the message of the cross is foolishness to those who are perishing..."

I looked to my right and a conflagration appeared in Ginger's eyes.

As I approached the coffin, the priest became silent and gestured downward. I looked in – it was completely empty!

The priest said, "Your bones have already disintegrated."

I started to ask him, "My bones?" when he motioned to the pews.

I looked back and the church was vacant; the churchgoers, Ginger and my parents had all disappeared.

Then I was seated at the Firenze Pakistani restaurant where my girlfriend was saying, "I want to sleep on the Ponte Vecchio bridge. How cool would that be? Even Hitler had respect for it and didn't destroy it when Axis troops were retreating. And I'd be able to paint the sunrise over the Arno."

I had finally force-swallowed the pieces of chicken bone and said, "I've been living in the Arno for some time now, down in the soft, thick, mud. Far beneath, where the crucian carp and sunfish swim."

Hey Badger

It was predetermined that Maria would mop the floor twice a week, never speak to strangers and be the exclusive changer of Josie's dirty diapers. Joel would sit rocking in his La-Z-Boy watching football from Sunday afternoon through Monday night, only briefly interrupted by sleep and work.

Every Wednesday evening Joel took Josie grocery shopping and Maria got an hour of downtime. It was then that she would get lost while staring into her stained-glass bedroom window and wonder how she had fallen into such a life. Not a dozen years ago, she regularly took shots with friends at bars' last calls and, sometimes, ended up in bed with random guys.

Then she met Joel.

He seemed open-minded and relatively modern. But soon after they got married, he interrogated her about where she went whenever she left the house, which had become increasingly rare. Even when she had been working, he listened closely for any holes in her stories and perk up his ears when male colleagues' names were mentioned. After she became pregnant with Josie, he convinced her to quit her job, at least until the child grew up.

Each time that Joel and Josie went to the store, Maria put on fresh, blood-red nail polish as a faint glimmer of the past. Joel complained that this was unnecessary, since she didn't go anywhere but, in the end, it was something he allowed. Maria would say that her going nowhere wasn't quite accurate, reminding him that she took Josie to the playground nearly every day when the weather cooperated. He gave a sullen nod, fretting about the young men who took their children there and mused that he should accompany Josie and Maria to the playground more often. Yet this was impossible. He worked during the day and in the evenings, there was SportsCenter followed by CBS News and *Homeland*. Saturday mornings didn't work either. He always had coffee with college friends, who also lived in the Chicago area, which often led to lunch.

One Tuesday evening, when Joel returned from the office, he found Josie in his playpen alone. Maria was nowhere to be found. He called out her name while darting through the house, searching every room. All he heard in response was the ever-increasing volume of Josie's wails. He finally picked up Josie; but Josie nearly flailed out of his arms.

The ripped-out piece of notebook paper on the kitchen table caught his eye. He picked it up and peered at it closely, as he always found difficulty deciphering Maria's handwriting.

It read: "Hey badger, I'm gone."

Connected

Amidst the fickle fat, Jeremy, an emerald wasp, learned how to navigate.

His mom, Theresa, had stung a cockroach's front thoracic ganglion, turning the beast's front legs into Jell-o. Then she hit the brain, petrifying the roach. The third sting went deep into its second thoracic ganglion, under the bug's armor, causing the roach to stretch out like a sunbather in paradise. That way Theresa could plant an egg on the roach's leg where, when hatched, her larvae would be in a perfect position to crawl up the roach's leg and chew through a weak part of its exoskeleton, so Jeremy could dwell inside the insect. Once there, the baby emerald wasp's bottle would be the roach's innards. When Jeremy became an adult, he'd break through the bug's body, leaving a dead roach in his wake.

But let's go back in time a bit, shall we?

Before he was born, Jeremy was on the right path. Theresa had solar sail wings and a stinger that was other wasps' envy. She learned how to fly at the Annapolis Naval Academy. Her husband, Jason, was a pint-sized, no-good manager who had authority over 100 no-good, nobody, male wasps.

When Theresa went at her target, to create a safe space where her child could gain nourishment and a natural, hands-on education inside a cockroach, things were looking up. Her no-good husband even hovered at a safe distance in front of the roach, to distract the beast. But because Jason had just come from gorging on a decomposing grape, he passed out in front of the roach. This left it up to Theresa to take care of things: in addition to planting an egg, she saved her husband from being feasted on by the roach.

Jeremy's host was plump and offered ample developmental nutrients until he came into his own. He'd soon become a strong wasp who knew how to maneuver, delicately praising his mother's wealthy friends and his no-good dad's higher-up colleagues without them ever realizing they were being buttered up.

Everyone said that Jeremy's future had a Miracle Whip throne in it. Some even thought that Jeremy might start his own Miracle Whip dynasty, where he could commandeer a few of the blue, red and white glass containers.

One of his dad's friends, no-good, pint-sized Mr. Rameses, sat on a Miracle Whip throne and Theresa often had Jeremy spend weekends with him. Mr. Rameses explained to Jeremy how he had nothing growing up. He didn't even have a roach to gorge on during childhood. He was nursed by his no-good dad and stinger mom who had nothing.

"You," he once told Jeremy, "are in luck. If you play your cards right, I'll pass my Miracle Whip crown onto you someday."

Theresa introduced Jeremy to several other important wasps, including Mathilde, a yogurt-eating fiend. She was known for her courage, especially when a human hand was about to crash down upon her and other emerald wasps as they imbibed yogurt. Mathilde was always the last to leave but continued to emerge unscathed.

Her secret – she told others – was to look humans in the eye and then, "they'll understand that you're someone, too, with full rights. They'll pause what they're doing and start talking to you."

But Theresa didn't buy it, so she decided to watch Mathilde feasting on a yogurt bed as a human hand came down towards her. As she watched, she saw that Mathilde never communicated with the human. Yet instead of flying directly towards the hand, as so many other frazzled wasps were apt to do, Mathilde scurried away (not using her wings at all!) to safety. For her bravery and cunning, she ruled over several yogurt cartons.

Mathilde also taught classes for elite wasps titled, "Self-actualizing your buzz" which Theresa made sure to enroll Jeremy in. In this course, Mathilde taught young emerald wasps how to mimic the buzz of bumblebees, honeybees and hornets.

"Once you acquire this buzz," she often reminded her class, "the world is your oyster."

Aside, she thought, "If only emerald wasps could incubate their larvae in oysters, then the world would be their whale."

When Jeremy began his career, approximately two months after emerging from the depleted roach, he used his connections to gain monopoly control over yogurt containers and Miracle Whip jars. He barely had to lift his wings and at least five other wasps would be at his side, asking how they could help. Jeremy hired security guards, created his own police force and employed AI coders who built robotic wasps to experiment with various methods of harvesting cockroaches.

Micky, a wasp who Jeremy had briefly met after emerging from the roach, asked Jeremy for a managerial position as a security guard. Micky looked like a cockroach, a wingless beast who had no sticky, spiderweb-like bonds to connected wasps. As Micky continued to pester Jeremy, he could no longer retain his rage. He ended up burying Micky alive in a fresh batch of whole milk yogurt in front of an audience, as it'd be a good learning experience for other emerald wasps.

When Jeremy died six long months later, he had lived longer than any emerald wasp on record. His friends transported yogurt to a countertop and had waterskiing competitions in his commemoration. Jeremy's body was held in a hollowed-out Miracle Whip container as a mausoleum, right beside the depleted carcass of the same roach that Jeremy was said to have harvested as a child.

Jeremy's children Henrietta and Maude never had to work a day in their life. They piggy backed on the funeral's yogurt-water skiing concept and had their underlings develop Jeremy theme parks. Yogurt skiing became the main attraction and Jeremy's smiling face, and convivial wink were omnipresent on all the rides.

Jeremy always told his children to stay ahead by always befriending the biggest wasp in the room. And, I suppose, he was right.

Tumbleweed

Marissa and Allie were on Flight 797 to Phoenix with plans to meet their mother, Tabatha, after five years of not seeing her. They were mad at her for not attending Allie's 2017 Bunker Hill Community College graduation. Tabatha had explained that was the time of year when she always visited Boca Raton, so there was nothing she could do. After a few years, the daughters' anger had waned, but Covid came along and upended plans of visiting Phoenix.

The sisters were seated beside each other on the plane. Marissa had to buy Allie dinner to get the window seat. To her chagrin, Allie was stuck between Marissa and an overweight man. Early in the flight, the man, who had taken the armrest between he and Allie, had fallen asleep. His upper body leaned increasingly into Allie's space, causing Allie and Marissa to become closer than they had been since they were children, when they would cuddle up together and watch early Saturday morning cartoons.

Tabatha waved from her rusty blue 2003 Toyota Camry as the sisters wheeled their luggage out of the airport. After hugging them both and kissing Allie on the cheek, Tabatha apologized for not attending her graduation. Allie looked down at her dark green Chuck Taylors.

Marissa said, "It's so hot out!"

"It's 105 degrees today."

Marissa's eyes widened and Tabatha pulled her sunglasses down, held up both of her arms and set her hands ajar.

"Climate change. Not my fault!"

Allie said, "But you moved here."

"The world turns, can't help if I move with it."

Marissa and Allie exchanged glances as they got into the car.

In minutes, they were flying on the freeway.

Allie leaned forward from the backseat and asked, "How fast are you going?"

Tabatha gestured to the speedometer. Marissa tilted her head sideways and peered at it.

"95!"

"Chill out. This isn't the land of the Puritans, where y'all live. Besides, the speed limit is 80 mph, and the roads are so straight out here."

They arrived at a restaurant in Cave Creek, a Phoenix suburb, for lunch. The place had dark brown, wooden walls, swinging double doors at the front, "Let's Go Brandon" signs covering the walls and a life-size replica of Donald Trump made of straw, with an extra orangey face, at the bar next to the cash register.

A waiter came over holding a notepad and said, "How're y'all doing? I'm Jason and will be your server this afternoon. Can I get you started with something to drink?"

Tabatha said, "The usual, Hunny."

When Allie and Marissa muttered that they only wanted water, the mother asked, "What's wrong with you two? You're on vacation, right?"

"It's just so early in the day, mom," said Marissa, eyeing Jason's leg tattoos as he walked away.

"That's why I left Massachusetts. Nothing personal, you know. It's just that kind of attitude and that by-the-book orderliness that I just can't handle."

159

Allie asked, "Isn't that all over this country?"

"No way! You have people here who take a sip of tequila for breakfast. It's not because they're alcoholics. They're just living, you know? They do what they feel like."

Marissa said, "Except get abortions."

"Can't have everything!"

The drinks arrived and Tabatha said, "Bottoms' up!" before drinking a half-filled, straight glass of Siete Leguas tequila.

"The water's warm," said Marissa.

"Hunny, they don't keep restaurants open by serving water. Get a real drink if you want it done right."

"Do you always drink so early in the day?" asked Allie.

"Come on, what's up with you guys? You're the young ones!"

They ordered food and Tabatha ordered another tequila.

"You didn't answer my question."

"About drinking? No, I don't, for your information. I'm seeing my two daughters after a long time. I'm celebrating! Ain't I got a right to celebrate?"

They shared nachos loaded with refried beans, sizzling Mexican cheese, jalapenos, olives, ground beef, salsa and two huge dollops of sour cream in the corners. Tabatha sipped her ever-replenished tequila, hardly eating anything, and Allie and Marissa ordered light beers to go with the food.

The daughters each had their mouths full when Tabatha leapt up, walked over and threw her arms around them.

"My babies! I'm so happy to see you guys!"

"Ok, mother," said Allie, pushing her mother's gangly arms away, "No need to get all PDA."

"Why not? I miss you guys. It's been way too long."

"You could've visited us. No one was stopping you."

"Well, I meant to, honestly. It was just one of those things that I never go around to."

"Because we aren't important enough. Got it."

"That's not true, Hunny. You girls are the world to me, you know that."

"Really? Then why didn't you come to my college graduation?"

"Are we still on that? I've told you time and again that's the time of year when I always go to Florida. I need vacations, too, Hunny."

"You hardly ever visited, even before that. You just don't care. Going to Florida was just an excuse that you had then."

Tabatha put her hand through her free-flowing graying black hair and stared at her empty tequila glass. "I'm Proud to be an American" blasted over the radio. Although the restaurant was empty when they arrived, it had become packed with the after-work crowd, causing a loud din of voices.

Tabatha's chest heaved and she started to break down into tears.

"You two always blame me for everything. Maybe I've done wrong...Please forgive me."

Allie stared at her and said, "We can't."

She got up and walked towards the door.

Marissa looked from her sister to her mother then followed Allie out, saying quietly, "Bye, Mom."

Tabatha went to the bathroom, dried her eyes and put on bright pink lipstick. She looked at herself in the mirror; her stare bounced back and forth for a million light years. She nodded solemnly to herself and left the restaurant.

She found Marissa and Allie standing by her blue Camry.

Marissa said, "Neither of us had reception to order an Uber. Can you give us a ride to the airport?"

"I'd be happy to, but…"

"But nothing," said Allie. "Just take us there and we'll pay you. Then you can go back to your life, and we'll get back to ours."

They drove in silence, past tall cacti and tumbleweeds blowing across the road.

"Desert wind," Tabatha said. "We don't get much of it but when we do, it's a real mother."

"The kind of mother like you?" said Allie, biting her lower lip.

Tabatha smiled, looking back at Allie through the rearview.

"Sort of."

They turned off the highway to the Phoenix Sky Harbor airport.

Tabatha took a deep breath, tried to meet their eyes and said, "Girls, I'm sorry that I'm a kind of a tumbleweed mother, blowing here, there and everywhere. When Rick and I had you guys, I wanted to be there for you. It was when you were both about ten years old that the pressure just became too much for me. The company I worked for started having me work on weekends and I was still on the clock late into the evening. After a year of that, I just broke down. I quit the job and left you all. I know you know that, but I don't think you ever knew why."

Marissa said, "I remember you leaving one day with a huge tan suitcase that had a diagonal, blue and white stripe across it. I got back from camp, and thought you were just heading off on a business trip or something."

"I knew that the bitch was leaving us then. You could see it in her eyes."

"I deserve that, I guess."

"You do deserve it."

"Come on, Allie. I'm not that bad. I hit a rough patch and bolted. We all make mistakes, Hunny."

Allie clenched her teeth. She put down the visor and looked at herself in the mirror and thought, "Don't give in. You do love her; still, don't cave this time…But you knew that she'd try to woo you over when you came to Arizona. Then why did you even bother coming?"

They pulled into the departure area, where cars and taxis were triple-parked, and traffic was backed up.

Tabatha found a place to live-park near the front entrance after a long wait.

The daughters had begun taking their luggage out from the trunk when Tabatha said, "I'm going to go with you guys!"

Marissa asked, "What? Why?"

"To prove to you both that I can still be a good mother, like I was when you were kids."

Allie said, "Were you ever? I don't remember that."

"I tried to be. We used to do stuff together, as a family."

Allie eyed a policewoman walking towards them. She looked at her mother and was blinded by the low evening sun.

The policewoman said, "You can't park here. Gotta move now!"

Allie pictured her mother and her, splashing each other in a kiddie pool and having a squirt-gun fight when they got out. Her mother chased her all around their small yard, squirting her on the scorching hot day. The dried-up, coarse grass, which had hurt her bare feet every day that summer, was no longer noticeable.

Then they were at a wildlife refuge and a park ranger yelled at four-year-old Allie for throwing a pebble into the marsh. Tabatha raged at the ranger, asking how he dared to raise his voice at her little girl. "Besides," Tabatha said, "the groundwater nearby is polluted but a pebble is going to harm the animals here? Come on!"

Allie looked at her mother arguing with the traffic cop. The cop was trying to pull luggage out of her hand and put it back into the car, saying that they had to go to the parking garage.

Tabatha said, "Get your hands off my daughter's luggage!"

"Ok, fine. Come with us!" said Allie, smiling.

They abandoned the 2003 Toyota in the parking garage and walked into the airport together.

Fresh Start

Boston's tall treehouses in the early December snow call to mind playing with building blocks as a kid. I'd stack them up high as I could while sitting on the wooden cellar floor, and outside the window, the snow piled high.

I'm in the passenger seat of the extended, white courier van as José drives. José is a bit older than me, in his mid-20s with a goatee. His delivery route has more than 120 stops around downtown, so he needs someone to run into the high-rise office buildings as the other person sits in the van to prevent it from getting a parking ticket. He starts work around 6 am and finishes at 6 pm, and for lunch gets a slice of pizza or a warm, toasted sandwich from some of the best hole-in-the-wall spots downtown.

The ride into the city takes an hour and a half in the traffic even though it's a seven mile drive. I become hypnotized by the windshield wipers' back and forth motion as we take deep hits from a blunt. I'm taken to times past – getting lost in Minnesota while driving in the *Master and Man* blizzard, Fiona breaking up with me when she thought she was pregnant and leaving the Prudential Center after work into the throng of people as they emerged from their offices.

I watch people on their commutes to work and begin to make up stories about each of them, wishing I had a notebook and pen. But I laugh to myself, knowing all that I see and think will be broiled in subterranean cauldrons and reappear in some later form, when I get home and sit at the typewriter.

Once downtown, José drives seamlessly through narrow streets flooded with people. He bears down with quick jabbing beeps that dissuade pedestrians from crossing and hurrying those in the middle of the street to the side. We park in an alleyway and smoke another blunt as he organizes the day's route. Then he hands me a bunch of payrolls to deliver to nearby buildings.

When I get into the elevator at the first stop, it is empty, so I write on the elevator wall: "None of this means anything. Speak up and be true or shut up and go to bed!" – one of Kerouac's best quotes.

I get out on the 23rd floor and enter a dimly lit, empty office. After turning the corner, I stand in front of a secretary without saying anything for a few seconds. She looks up startled, shakes her head, before signing for the delivery.

Back in the elevator, I start to write, "Everyone is dead. Wake the hell up! Get out of your coffins!"

A man enters wearing a blue sport coat and a tie with a briefcase in hand, peering at me as I put away my pen.

"You know, I used to do that sort of thing. Actually, I was more into graffiti. I traveled to West Berlin and wrote on the Wall there: "The Wall is only in your head.""

I nod.

And now you're working in this coffin every day. You chose to die. Nice work.

Snow has begun to race down. The wind carries it in pockets, swirling the cold white through channels between buildings and hitting pedestrians sideways. It sneaks through the top of my jacket and falls down my back.

When I get into the van, the engine is still running with the heat on full blast, but José isn't there. I look outside, watching morning rush hour people speeding along to work, seeming to curse the snow beneath their breath. For some reason they appear surprised - like they didn't realize that it would snow in Boston again this winter as it always does.

I look up to the high treehouses on either side, probably at least 70 stories tall, and watch as more lights turn on inside.

A meter maid taps on the window. She looks younger than me, maybe either 19 or 20. She has long curly black hair, dark-rimmed glasses and deep, warm brown eyes. Her firm gaze fades when our eyes meet and her white teeth mirror the falling snow, contrasting with her light brown complexion.

"You have to move."

"It's so cold out. Do you have to stay outside all day?"

"Not at lunch!" She says, her lips slowly curling into a smile.

"I'm waiting for my co-worker. But I can move for you...maybe you and I could get lunch."

She blushes, looking down at the yellow citation booklet in her hand.

"Hmm...I don't know. I kind of don't know you at all. You could be a murderer."

"I am. But I only kill the dead."

Her eyes widen but then she begins to smile.

"Seriously. I mean, why would I just get lunch with a random guy...a guy who should get a ticket?"

"Why not though, right? Better than eating lunch alone!"

"How do you know I eat lunch alone? I usually have lunch with Donny."

"Donny? Your boyfriend?"

"Yeah, my sexy boyfriend, Don Rumsfeld."

We laugh.

"Ok, fine, we'll get lunch. You know Priscilla's Pastry on Milk Street? They have amazing, melted sandwiches. And they have this crazy-good African peanut soup."

"Sounds delicious. I'll bring an umbrella for you."

"Umbrellas don't do anything against the snow!"

I put my hand out the window and set it ajar. She starts to reach out to it but quickly pulls her hand back.

*

Priscilla's Pastry is half underground, with a long rectangular window that allows patrons to look out and see Bostonians' feet as they pass. Jackie, the meter maid, texted me that this place is for the mail carriers, couriers and meter maids – the office types don't bother to come in. However, it is very much a café, with several different types of coffee, cappuccino, soups and warm, freshly made bread. There are bookshelves along each wall with newspapers, magazines, a few books and a bunch of games, including cards, Viking and Celts chess pieces and Scrabble, for workers to play on their breaks. Lester Young's slow, sleepy tenor sax music curls through the cigarette smoke, which pervades throughout the room, though smoking was made illegal in Boston last summer. On the window ledge, there is a globe with Soviet bloc countries still on the map.

Jackie leans over from outside. She peers down and catches my eyes, indicating that she'll be in shortly.

A few minutes later, she sits across from me, unfurling a black woolen scarf with purple and orange pumpkins on it, takes off her mittens that left her fingertips bare and removes her snug hat.

We order coffees and pressed sandwiches, but instead of eating, conversation engulfs us.

It's weird – as we start talking, I have the feeling that I've known her all my life. We talk while slowly sipping our scalding coffees.

I learn that she takes art history courses at Bunker Hill Community College at night but is bored with them; she says they aren't challenging enough. Her older brother, who had looked out for her after their parent's divorce, was sent to Afghanistan the previous winter to fight Al Qaeda. He enlisted the day after 9/11. Her grandmother, who immigrated from the Dominican Republic, stays awake every night thinking about him. The grandma says that at least it's a quick path to citizenship. Jackie was born here, so she doesn't have to worry about that.

It turns out that Jackie is a painter of the surrealist school. Though Jackie doesn't appreciate the 20th-century surrealist art as much as impressionism, she reads surrealist literature, like poems from Rene Char, Andre Breton's *Nadja* and really digs Antonin Artaud's Theater of Cruelty. As she puts it, the theater of cruelty pushes the audience, through terror, directly into the play, excising them from their lives. When they return to their lives after the play is over, they'll never see things the quite same way again. They'll be shaken, jolted, as if hit with a lightning bolt, from their stultified lives. She tells me that no one in her community and none of her friends get her. I commiserate, saying that's basically the same for me.

José taps on the window from outside and motions to me to head back out. I indicate one more minute, but he seems impatient, so I go and talk to him. He tells me that I can just see her later today or on the weekend. But I don't want to. I want to see her now and be with her nonstop. He says that he'll give me five minutes, so I go back inside. Jackie looks at her watch, and says she has to get back to work soon, too.

"What if we both just said *fuck it*?" I ask.

"I don't think that'd fly with my boss."

"Yeah, but what if we said, 'so what'?"

"Like 'so what' to our jobs? I do that all the time. But 'so what' to getting fired? That's a completely different story."

"To both!"

"You're crazy! I can't do that. I've got bills to pay."

"You could get a job somewhere else."

"Why? I have a job here."

Outside José blares the horn.

174

"Because...I don't know...let's just go somewhere and start fresh."

"But I just met you."

Stress marks appear on her forehead; she takes a deep breath and looks outside.

"Is that your van beeping?"

"Yup. But I don't care!"

"Look. Don't get me wrong. It's not like I don't want to see you again. But to take off, just like that?"

"Why not? Do you like being a meter maid? I'm sure you could do that anywhere. Or we could move somewhere else, and you could start fresh as a painter. I told you that I'm a writer – we both could start fresh."

Jackie peers down at her coffee mug and, with the stirrer, fishes at a few coffee grounds stuck on the side. She looks up slowly with a burgeoning smile and takes the globe down from the window ledge.

"Spin it! Wherever my finger ends up, we'll go."

As I spin the globe, her pointer finger stops in the middle of the Pacific Ocean, about 500 miles north of Hawaii. I spin again. This time it stops way up in the Canadian Arctic.

"Do people even live way up there?" she asks.

"Maybe some Inuit people."

"Ok, one more try! If I land in the middle of nowhere again, when we leave this café, we'll never meet each other again. Ever. But we could both just leave right now, see each other again soon and stay here in Boston."

"Let's spin for it!" I say, whirling the globe around as fast as possible.

As she closes her eyes, the fading early afternoon light falls onto her face. She moves her finger up and down the twirling globe like a fortune teller.

When it stops, her finger lands directly on Tokyo.

She doffs her meter maid hat and takes out her notebook from her jacket pocket, placing it on top of her uneaten sandwich.

We leave the café together, walking right past the courier van. José sits there gawking at us.

Acknowledgements

"Fresh Start" in *Phoenix Z Publishing*, May 2023 issue.

"Hey Badger" in *Quail Bell Magazine*, January 12, 2023.

"Nanny" and "Dump" in *Synchronized Chaos*, December 15, 2022.

"Home, At Last" in *Dumpster Fire Press*, November 2022 issue.

"The Special Suite" in *Impspired*, Issue 18, August 2022.

"The Broadcaster" in *Impspired*, Issue 18, August 2022.

"The Tenants" in *Kolkata Arts*, July 3, 2022.

"The Piece of Red Hair" in *Kolkata Arts*, July 3, 2022.

"Deletion" in *Synchronized Chaos*, July issue, 2022.

"A Curious Hospital" in *Pinecone Review*, Issue 4, June 2022.

"Latitude or longitude?" in *Fresh Words: An International Literary Magazine*, Volume 2, Number 3, June 2022.

"Connected" in *Bombfire*, 2/8/2022.

"Alissa" in *Lothlorien Poetry Journal*, 1/15/2022.

"Jesus's Bloody Nose" in *Angel Rust*, Issue 4, October 2021.

"Formorians" in *Digging Through the Fat*, Issue 13, 11/18/2020.

"Character and Author" in *Pif Magazine*, Issue 277, June 2020.

"Polarization" in *The Opiate*, Fall 2019, Volume 19.

"The Initials" in *Bitchin' Kitsch*, volume 11, October 2019/*Adelaide Literary Award Anthology 2019: Short stories* (Finalist).

"Platypus" in *Adelaide Literary Magazine*, Number 25, June 2019.

"The New Employee" in *Work Literary Magazine*, 8/27/2018.

"flushing bullshit" in *The Opiate*, Fall 2018, Volume 15.

"That Night" in *34th Parallel*, Issue 54 (July 2018).

About the Author

As a prolific author from the Boston area, Peter F. Crowley writes in various forms, including short fiction, op-eds, poetry and academic essays. In 2020, his poetry book 'Those Who Hold Up the Earth' was published by Kelsay Books and received impressive reviews by Kirkus Review, the Bangladeshi New Age and two local Boston-area newspapers. His writing can be found in Middle East Monitor, Znet, 34th Parallel, Pif Magazine, Galway Review, Digging the Fat, Adelaide's Short Story and Poetry Award anthologies (finalist in both) and The Opiate.

His poetry book *Empire's End*, to be published by Alien Buddha Press, is due out in the late 2023 summer.

Made in the USA
Middletown, DE
26 September 2023